"I can't spend county money on a hunch. I need more proof than that."

Maggie seethed. "Then listen to the tape. Who is that?" She pointed to the tape still in the sheriff's hand.

The sheriff sighed and then looked at the tape he'd taken from her. "But we can listen to it. I think we still have a tape player around here." He dug in a drawer and came up with a hand-held dictation machine. "This might work."

"I also have something else. When the lake water receded, I hiked down where you discovered the boat, and I found this buried in mud. It is Jeff's commuter cup. He always carried it, and it must have fallen out of the boat. The lid was still on it. When I opened it, the liquid was still in there, and it smells really bad. Not like something Jeff would drink. I mean, Jeff was a drinker, but this doesn't smell like bourbon. He only drank beer and bourbon. He was a picky drunk. And I have had a bad feeling about his death from the beginning. He wouldn't get drunk and just fall out of his boat. He grew up around the water. And this isn't bourbon." Maggie felt as if a weight had been lifted off her shoulders when she finished what she had to say.

Praise for Peggy Chambers

"Whether you're reading for true escape or just a few moments of entertainment, Peggy Chambers has the book for you.

In Blooming Greed she tells an engaging tale of life and death in the small town community of Mannford, OK on Keystone Lake. With a brief description she will draw you in with her ability to paint scenes of great detail and personalities so genuine they feel familiar...like memories with old friends.

The Keystone series will leave you longing for another update from your friends at the lake."

~ *Shelley Singleton, Avid Reader*

Blooming Greed

by

Peggy Chambers

The Keystone Lake Series Book 2

Blooming Greed

Contact Information: info@thewildrosepress.com

Cover Art by *Kim Mendoza*

The Wild Rose Press, Inc.
PO Box 708
Adams Basin, NY 14410-0708
Visit us at www.thewildrosepress.com

Publishing History
First Edition, 2022
Trade Paperback ISBN 978-1-5092-4025-8
Digital ISBN 978-1-5092-4026-5

The Keystone Lake Series Book 2
Published in the United States of America

Dedication

I want to dedicate this book to our good friends at Keystone Lake. Thank you for the time we played on the island and sat around the campfire at night. Those memories will last a lifetime.

Thanks go out to Russel N. Singleton, Attorney at Law, for his help in the legalities of this book.

I also want to thank Justin H. Smither, Assistant Lake Manager, Keystone/Heyburn/Arcadia Lakes, US Army Corps of Engineers, Tulsa District for his help with seeing the dam in my mind's eye.

Chapter 1

Jeff Larson was drunk again. He'd filled the ice chest with beer for both him and the buddy who backed out tonight. Jeff always carried a little extra just in case. But since he was alone, there was no danger of running out. He knew drinking was the one thing he could count on in his life. It was his constant companion—and wouldn't leave him like some other things.

Of course, he also knew he needed to quit. Lots of people had told him so, and deep down he believed them, but he doubted he ever would. He told himself he would slow down, keep it in check. He talked to himself every day, but he never seemed to get through the day without a drink—or several.

And that was all right with him.

He stared out into the darkening sky above the lake he'd loved since a child. It wasn't always a lake. The Cimarron and Arkansas rivers had been dammed to create it. The old Yachee Native American tribe used to live where the lake was now. Later Keystone Lake was named after the small town of Keystone, really just a post office, in the early 1900s. It was so named because it was a key position between the two rivers. When it was flooded, the former town sites of Mannford, Prue, Appalachia, and part of Osage also were abandoned to make room for the lake. Jeff had lived on the lake all his life and was an amateur history buff. He learned all he could about the place he loved.

The little motor on the back of the boat coughed twice and then ground to a halt. "Damn thing," he said out loud to no one in particular. "I knew I needed to get this motor in for a checkup, and now it's almost dark. I'll be stuck out here for hours." He looked up, his eyes catching lightning in the distance. There were a few clouds in the sky but no storms in the forecast tonight. He'd checked before he left home. The rain had been relentless this spring.

He reached into the tackle box for a flashlight, then tilted the little outboard motor up to see if he could find what was wrong. But first he needed another drink. Thank goodness the buddy who bailed on him tonight had handed him the commuter cup at the dock before he gave his excuses. Jeff almost left the cup and its contents sitting there. The beer in the ice chest was fine for fishing. But he needed what was in the commuter cup if he was fixing a motor. Just to steady his nerves.

"What else can go wrong tonight?" he grumbled, moving again toward the end of the boat. He guessed he'd never get to the dam on time. He'd contact the guy at the Corps of Engineers in the morning and apologize for not meeting him. It had taken some time to get the meeting in the first place—the engineer was new to the dam—and meeting him after hours was not what the guy wanted to do.

Zebra mussels were probably clogging up the engine. He usually washed the boat and motor dutifully each time it was pulled from the water. But lately, it just sat in the marina waiting for another fishing trip. Zebra mussels were invading the whole lake. They were everywhere. Rumor had it they were the culprit that was tearing up the aging dam. A fact he was going to talk to the Corps about. This was his lake, and he wasn't going to let something so little as a zebra mussels take it from him.

Earlier, it had been the algae bloom that was the problem. It happened when they had a drought. But Mother Nature had a way of leveling things out. First a drought, and now so much rain the lake was flooded. At least the algae bloom had disappeared. But it would be back as soon as the water levels dropped again. It was always something when you lived on a lake.

All in all, the lake Jeff grew up on was in trouble.

Unscrewing the lid, he took a long drag on the cup then screwed the lid back on tightly—grimacing. Lord, that tasted bad. But no need to waste good booze by spilling it. He'd want it later. Swallowing, he set the cup in the bottom of the boat and stuck the end of the flashlight in his mouth. He would need both hands free to check out the little motor. He reached for the screwdriver in the toolbox he always kept in the boat. A wave of nausea rolled over him, and he grabbed his stomach without thinking. The plastic flashlight he held in his teeth suddenly tasted metallic, and the pain in his gut became worse. He needed a bathroom, and there wasn't one out here. He'd drank a lot of beer, but it never upset his stomach—he was used to it.

Unexpectedly, he knew he was going to vomit. The feeling came on suddenly and violently. Dropping the flashlight, he leaned over the side of the boat much too fast. The small metal boat leaned quickly, and gravity pulled his body sideways. Then abruptly he slid over the side and into the water. The body emptied his stomach of its contents. And gagging he inhaled making him gulp water instead of air. He reached out and grabbed the side of the boat, but pain contorted his body again, and he wrapped his arms around his belly. Another convulsion, and he sucked lake water into his mouth and lungs.

This couldn't be happening. He couldn't drown, he knew too much about the water. Trying to control his lungs, he held on to what air he still had left. Unable to release the hold he had on his stomach and use his arms to pull to the surface, he felt himself sinking slowly. He was aware of the water rushing over him as he sank toward the refuse left on the bottom by the zebra mussels. Finally, his lungs felt they would burst from lack of air. He tried desperately not to gasp.

But Mother Nature took over and, instinctively, his body inhaled.

Chapter 2

Jolted awake from a sleep that had been a long time coming, Maggie Beck realized the persistent banging came from her back door. Someone knocked on her door in the middle of the night—or was it early morning before daylight? Groggy, she shuffled to the kitchen pulling on her robe. Maybe her brother forgot his keys.

The uniform was the first thing she saw and knew instinctively why he was there. Jeff was several hours overdue and didn't answer his cell phone. She hadn't called anyone yet, hoping she wouldn't have to ask her neighbors for help. He was probably drinking again. She didn't want the embarrassment of sending someone to look for him only to find him passed out in the little metal boat floating lazily along as mosquito bait.

"I'm sorry to disturb you so early, Mrs. Beck, but I'm afraid I have some bad news about Jeff." Sheriff Niles Montgomery came around to the back door on the deck that faced the water. Anyone who knew the Becks knew they never used the front door. She held on to the cabinet top so hard she was afraid she would leave dents in the tile. She was terrified of the news she was about to hear and thought maybe if he didn't speak, it would all turn out to be just a bad dream. So, she interrupted him to keep him from speaking.

"Would you like some coffee, Sheriff?" she asked wiping the sleep from her eyes.

"No thank you, ma'am, why don't you sit down, you look a little pale." It sounded more like an order than a request. The voice of authority. She sat immediately.

"I'm sorry to have to tell you this, but Jeff was found in the water this evening on Sandy Beach. He apparently drowned. We found the boat a few miles downstream. We've taken him to the coroner's to make a complete determination of cause of death." He took a deep breath. "I'm really very sorry. Is Paul home?" The sheriff looked around the room like he expected another soul to appear. "Is there someone I could call for you? Someone you could stay with?"

Wishing her husband, Paul, was home, Maggie shook her head. "No, Jeff couldn't just drown. He's lived around this lake all his life. Something must have happened. Was he alone?"

The sheriff raised his eyebrows in question. "As far as we know."

Maggie always begged her brother to wear his life jacket. Even if he was a strong swimmer. He would be fine, he told her. He knew what he was doing. Men always thought they knew what they were doing.

"Jeff promised he was not going to be out in deep water. Just staying in the cove. You found him on the other side of the lake?" Why, she wondered. Jeff might have been a drunk, but he wasn't stupid. She thought she could ask that a million times and never find the answer.

"Yes, ma'am. And the boat a little farther down. Maybe he drifted out more than he planned."

Maggie knew the islands disappeared due to the recent flooding, but people who knew the lake could still find them. They would show up again as soon as the water went down. And that was where the fish were biting. Jeff might have gone there, but not in that boat, and not by himself. It was a thirty-minute trip to the islands, and the water was too deep and choppy for such a small boat. But across from the islands at the beach they loved when they were kids was where they found him, face down in the debris brought about because of recent flooding. There really wasn't a beach there anymore, at least not until the water receded.

"A camper came upon the body and called 911 for help." The sheriff adjusted his belt.

"Was he already dead?" Maggie had no idea why she asked that question.

"There were no lights or sirens; there was no reason to hurry." The sheriff shuffled from one foot to the other looking uncomfortable. "Will you be okay?"

Maggie thought it must be hard to give people bad news all the time. But it went with the job. "Paul is out of town on business. But I'll be fine, Sheriff, really. Thank you. Do I need to identify his body?" She kept talking to stifle the flood of tears she knew was coming.

"No, ma'am, that won't be necessary. Everyone around here knew Jeff. Could I fix you a cup of tea or something? How about a glass of water?"

Before she could speak, the phone rang. News traveled fast in small towns. Maggie remembered stepping to the phone and hearing Allison say she would be right over. She didn't remember standing.

Maggie paced the kitchen with the phone in her hands thinking how to tell her husband and the children. It didn't occur to her to ask how, or what, or any of the normal questions. Paul and the kids would need to be told, and she had no idea how she would do that.

"I'll be fine, Sheriff," she said again. "My friend

Allison Wells is coming over to be with me. You don't have to stay any longer." She hung up the phone when she realized it was still in her hands. Allison had called the home phone. Maybe it was because it was late at night and the cell might be silenced.

"That's good, Mrs. Beck. No one should be alone at a time like this. But if it's all the same to you, I'll wait until she gets here."

It was all the same to Maggie. She had drifted off into her own little world again. It was something that always annoyed her friends and family.

The grandfather clock in the living room ticked away the minutes. It was the only noise in the house as Maggie and the sheriff sat in uncomfortable silence. Maggie jumped when a second knock sounded.

"I'll get it," Sheriff Montgomery said opening the door.

Allison flew in, engulfing Maggie and holding her in her arms. It wasn't until that moment Maggie started to cry. It was as if she was waiting for something to make this whole thing seem real to her. And Allison was that thing.

As the tears flowed, Maggie wondered what Jeff might have gone through just before he drowned. Did he know he was drowning? Was he aware of his fate, or did he just doze off and not wake up? What happened, and why was he dead? She suddenly felt she needed to see him for herself.

"Allison, will you take me to the coroner's, please? I need to see Jeff." Maggie stood and turned to go to the bedroom to change clothes.

The sheriff still looked embarrassed about being there, but he cleared his throat and spoke. "Mrs. Beck, why don't you wait until the funeral home has him? I think it would be much easier on you if you would wait."

"I agree," said Allison. "We'll go see him in the morning when Dermott's has him ready. You don't need to see him now. I'll stay with you tonight."

Just like that, the decisions were made for her. Ordinarily she hated when others made her decisions, but tonight, she didn't care.

"Tomorrow," she said, nodding her head.

Chapter 3

"Dammit!" Toni Stone wiped away the stain of street taco from her navy suit jacket. Erin Sampson and her aunt sat in the kitchen of the law office of Cronkite and Associates eating take-out lunch. "I've got a hearing this afternoon." She stood and walked to the sink wetting a paper towel and dabbing at the barely noticeable spot on her lapel.

"Yeah, that's what will rile up the judge, Toni, not you." N. Robert Cronkite, Bobby to those who knew him, said with a wink at Erin. He was the original partner at the firm. He and Toni were not only partners at the law firm, but they were also friends. And years ago, he'd taken Erin under his wing. Erin knew she was lucky to be working in his shadow, and that of her aunt's. She learned from them daily, and they often had lunch in the breakroom together.

"It looks fine, Aunt Toni. You can hardly see it. No one will notice." Erin watched her aunt walk back to the table. An elegant woman, she could be fierce as a tiger when cornered. And if she went into the courtroom annoyed today, Lord help the opposing counsel.

"Well, I guess it will have to do. If that's the only thing that irritates the judge, my day will be a breeze." Toni shoved the last bite of taco in her mouth and threw the paper plate in the trash.

Erin tried to hide a smile at the woman she loved

like a second mother. Aunt Toni was her mother's sister, and the three women had always been close. Aunt Toni often helped her mother and another friend drink a pitcher of margaritas on the weekend when Erin was growing up. Erin drank soda but always helped eat Toni's famous homemade guacamole. Aunt Toni loaned her a dress for the prom and never even flinched when it was ruined by the brute she went out with that night. Aunt Toni was there for her when Erin's mom fell ill and spent time in the hospital while Erin was still in college. And it was Aunt Toni who took on the richest man in Tulsa when Erin's best friend, Bernadette, was kidnapped by his son. Aunt Toni was her hero—and she was also her boss.

Toni walked to the sink and washed her hands then dried them on the paper towel. "Erin, I'd like you to look into something for me. The firm represents Sunset Hills Homeowners' Association on the lake. They have a concern that might bear looking into. I'll forward all my info to you, and you can get the working file from my assistant. They're worried about all the properties that are selling lately and want someone to look into it. See who's buying up all the land. They think something shady might be happening."

"Property sales around the lake seems normal during the spring with all the rain we've been having. I mean if your property floods, and you can't use it, sell it if you can. I would think that the sale of land could be a God-send when times are tough." Erin took her plate to the trash. The street tacos at the little café down the street were always good. She wished she and Rob could make some as tasty. She'd ask the cook for his recipe.

Toni stood at the doorway of the kitchen getting

ready to go back to her office. “That would be true if they were selling at appraised value. But they aren’t. They’re selling for pennies on the dollar. Let me know what you find out. Gotta go help out a client.” She smiled at her niece and turned walking down the hall.

Bobby followed her but first nodded to Erin. “Have a good afternoon, kiddo.”

He still called her that even after she passed the bar. He probably always would. But she knew he meant it in the best of ways. He was a father figure and a mentor, and she was pleased to work for him.

Erin had lived in the little town of Mannford, Oklahoma all her life with her mother who managed a flower shop. Her dad, a trucker, died in an accident when Erin was ten, and that left her and her mother to take on the world together. Though they missed him terribly, they did fine, especially with her Aunt Toni around. Erin and her mother had a wonderful relationship, but Erin longed to be more like her aunt. She knew the financial struggles of trying to make a living running a flower shop. When times were tough, people didn’t buy flowers.

When she grew up, she knew she wanted to be a lawyer like her aunt. So, after graduating high school, she secured a scholarship to TU. She moved to the big city of Tulsa and began working for Cronkite and Associates, her aunt’s law firm. It was part time at first while attending classes and full time in the summers. Within three years, Erin was able to begin the TU law school with the accelerated bachelor’s program. After passing the Bar Exam, she was hired in the same firm where she’d worked during college. Some called her lucky. She was. But she worked hard for her aunt and the firm, and she was determined to make partner someday like Aunt Toni.

She stopped by Toni's tastefully decorated office on the way back to her own. Erin was sure the artwork was original and she admired the cherry wood furniture and handwoven rug on the floor. She picked up the file from the assistant and then returned to her rather shabby desk. Salary as an associate wasn't like the salary of a partner. Someday she'd make better money and not have to sit at a used desk she found stored in the basement of the ancient building they occupied. She and Rob had moved it upstairs one weekend after getting permission to use it. After a little furniture polish, it shone like the tiny bit of sun that sometimes filtered in her alley-view window. Her one and only window had a telephone pole in the middle of it making it dark most days. But she was too busy to look out the window most of the time anyway. Opening the file, she began the investigation.

Her phone buzzed. "I have Bernadette Larson on the phone for you." Annette, the receptionist crooned into the phone. Erin liked her. She was a big improvement over the one before who tried to stab her in the back for being the niece of a partner.

"Thanks, Annette." Erin picked up the phone to talk to her best friend in the world—next to Rob. "Hey, lady, what's up?"

"Hi. I have some ideas for wedding dresses to show you and some swatches. What are you doing this evening?"

Bernadette, who had always had a flare for clothing trends, had gone into fashion design in college. Now she was attempting to create her own line of clothing at home with online sales. And she would have killed Erin if she had purchased an off-the-rack wedding dress for herself and her bridesmaids.

"I don't have a thing tonight. In fact, it's my night to cook, so I was thinking of ordering a pizza. Want to join us? Rob will probably be working in the living room anyway, so we can go in the bedroom and talk."

"Great. I'll bring what I have, and we'll try to not get pizza on them. By the way, lately I've been thinking of the color of peacocks. Maybe some teal, blue, and green for the bridesmaids' dresses. In fact—"she paused and inhaled "—maybe the real thing at the reception. Peacocks strolling the grounds during the reception. So artsy!"

Erin cleared her throat. "Not to mention peacock poop all over the place for the guests to step in. Peacock colors sound great, but no birds. Besides the reception is indoors, it will be winter, remember?" It was a good idea to keep Bernadette on a short leash sometimes. Her ideas could get a little out there.

"Okay, no birds, but I think you'll love the colors. See you after work," Bernadette said and quickly clicked off.

Erin didn't know what she'd do without her best friend. The woman was incredibly talented and could make clothing out of a pillowcase look good. She didn't normally make formal attire, but that didn't stop her from trying.

Getting back to business, Erin knew she still had a few hours and several cases to look at before going home and talking about wedding plans.

Checking out Toni's emailed computer file on the homeowners' association, she flipped open the folder on her desk and began to look into what had already been done. It didn't take long to see that the homeowners' association might have a viable gripe.

Chapter 4

Ted Shipley looked out onto the lake, his sandy blond hair lightly blowing in the wind. Shading his piercing blue eyes, he stared into the distance. From up on the dam, he could see for miles. He smiled as he observed the peninsula. If you knew where it was located, under all that water, it was a beautiful place. And he knew. Lots of natural sand washed into the area from the Cimarron and Arkansas Rivers and formed beaches—when the water was at normal levels. The peninsula would soon be his, and the resort he planned would be the most magnificent the area had ever seen.

He rubbed his hand over the cardboard tube that held the blueprints for the resort. He'd brought them from the architect he'd sworn to secrecy that morning. He planned to find a place to leave them at the dam, knowing he couldn't take them home. The cabinet just inside the door to the massive dam should hold the tube until he was ready to present them to the builder. When the time was right, he'd take them with him to the bank, along with the deeds to the property he owned. Then it wouldn't be long before he was a rich man.

But he wouldn't be the only one. The small town of Mannford would boom as people from Tulsa, and maybe even surrounding states, came to visit. He had big plans, and they were shortly coming to fruition. He just had to wait a little longer, and he could buy the rest of the area around it. No one wanted land that flooded all the time. It would go for rock bottom prices. Then once he owned it, he could control the dam and keep it from flooding. It would be up to the Corps of Engineers to replace the dam once his resort was up and running. That was going to have to happen eventually to protect his property and the rest of the lake.

When he came to town eight years ago, he knew this place could be his dream come true. The little realty company who hired him right after he got his license provided a small amount of money, but he needed more. Once he got to town it didn't take long for him to run into Hope. She was just the kind of woman he needed, quiet, unassuming, and a great mother. Not the kind of woman who would get in his way but would look good on his arm at social gatherings. She was everything he needed. He needed a woman who didn't ask questions.

The uniformed man wiped the sweat from his dark brow as he checked the gauges one more time. Sometimes he needed the stool to reach the ones up high. His employment with the Corps of Engineers was ending. Shipley told him soon he would work for the man who owned all the land around the dam. His days of working for small change were almost over.

"The dam can't take much more of this stress. The doors should open more easily. I told that to the committee. It needs repair. But no one listened. Now the whole place is flooded and, even with permission to let out more water, I can't do it fast enough. But you know that." He stepped down from the stool and walked to the other end of the room.

"It won't be long now, Decker. Just keep it running for a little bit longer. And let it out like we planned."

Shipley wondered if his employee really knew his job, but he feigned confidence. After all, he had no one else with the experience to do the job. Once the old dam came down and a new one was built, Decker could be expendable.

"I hope you know what you're doing, buying all this land around here. You know this dam is in bad shape and needs repair. We can't depend on it to hold forever. Maybe you should wait on the new dam before building the resort." The short worker adjusted the dial and checked the others to his right. "By the way, I got those zebra mussels dumped as close to the dam as possible last night. I thought you'd want to know. That's not going to make the dam any easier to control. But I guess you know that, too."

"I know what I'm doing. But it won't be much longer. You worry about the dam, and I'll worry about the price of land. We're going to make a killing. Just you wait and see." He carefully pulled the blueprints from the cardboard tube he'd carried in with him and looked once again at his dream. The dream of owning the biggest hotel ever to grace the shores of this man-made lake. And he would be its owner. It was a dream of his since he was young, and it was finally happening. He placed the blueprints back in the cardboard tube and then shoved it in the cabinet closing the door.

T & H Realty was all part of his master plan. He was a realtor and could only work for his boss for so long. It was time he branched out. Ted Shipley was proud of his accomplishments buying up the left-over land around the lake, but none so much as the latest purchase. The bank said he was cut off until he started to show a profit, but he was sure he could get the last tiny bit of land for a song—and he had the money for that. Now, if the owners would just sell. And why not? It wasn't like they could use the land anymore. It was almost underwater, and the trailer that sat there was ruined. They never visited anyway. Weekend people.

It was probably time he clued Hope in on his plans. She was the H in T & H Realty even though she didn't know it. She was too busy with the kids these days to know what he did or why. But he still loved her and wanted to provide for her and the kids. And if he didn't take some chances, they would never make a buck. Five kids to raise and educate took a lot of money—money he didn't have. But he would as soon as his ship came in. He liked that analogy with lake property. Okay maybe it was his boat that was coming in since the lake wasn't big enough to accommodate a ship. But if this worked out like he planned he could go on to bigger things.

Shipley opened the door and surveyed the land one more time before walking out and leaving for dinner.

Standing on the dock of the marina he waited on the burger he ordered for his food. Pier 51, the little floating restaurant with a gift shop and gas station for boats, had some of the best burgers around. When he got things up and running, he would talk to the owner of this place about joining him. His sandy blond hair blew back from his face showing remarkable blue eyes. His tall thin frame made him still appear young even though he was pushing forty—middle age he thought—middle age if he lived to be eighty, and that was a stretch with his family history. There wasn't a lot of longevity in his family. His father died young, a broken man in the grips of poverty. He left his wife and kids to fend for themselves. Ted knew poverty, and he never wanted to see it again. He swore to himself his children would not have to go to school in hand-me-down clothes while their mother worried how she would feed them. No, not his kids. They would survive—and do it in style. But first he had to get the last holdouts to sell that worthless bit of property. He made them a great offer on a piece of land that was flooding. The water crept closer to their little weekend mobile home every day and was not going down if he had anything to say about it.

And he did.

Chapter 5

Traffic was horrendous most mornings as commuters from bedroom communities drove into Tulsa. But this morning it was inevitable since she was running late. Ryan Windler was stuck in traffic and unable to move. She had to get downtown for work. She knew she needed to leave her hometown of Mannford earlier, but the alarm didn't go off this morning, or the coffee pot didn't work, or maybe it was her unruly hair. One way or another, she left the house later than she planned. The expressway was gridlocked, and the chances of being at work on time were zero. She glanced at the exit lane beside her and knew it would get her nowhere fast. She'd tried that before.

At least she wasn't in the car wreck that caused the traffic accident. She had something to be thankful for.

She turned up the music and checked her lipstick in the mirror as she seat-danced. A little morning groove might make the wait seem shorter. She dug through her purse looking for powder for a shiny nose. Her quick makeup job this morning looked like it in the morning light.

He eased up beside her from the outside lane that was closing and gunned the engine. What was he doing over there? Could he not see the merge sign? Cute guy in a red Ferrari. That just sounded like trouble. He smiled, and she smiled back trying not to. Men were not a good idea. Not that she didn't like them—oh she did—it was just that she never chose wisely. Mom was constantly on her case about when she would marry again—and have kids this time. Mom might have to depend on her sister for grandkids. Marriage was not something she even wanted to think about again. The last time was a disaster, and she was still not over it. She might be over him, but still mourned for the whole fairytale marriage thing.

The Ferrari guy smiled again and winked this time, keeping her from noticing the space that developed between her and the car ahead as it expanded. Then the Ferrari flew around and in front of her barely missing her bumper. She slammed on the brakes as he exited the freeway causing several horns to honk and tires to squeal as the sports car wove in and out of traffic.

"Jerk!" she yelled.

He threw her a wave. She thought about returning the wave, but with only her middle finger. Good riddance, she thought, not that she wouldn't have loved a ride in his expensive sports car. But his kind were never worth it. Suddenly the traffic started to move, slowly at first, but at least it was moving, and she joined the pack of already tired commuters who were just beginning their day.

Ryan pulled into the parking garage to her assigned place fifteen minutes late. One thing about the accounting firm, she wouldn't have to fight for a parking place. The firm rented exactly the right amount, and everyone had their own. It balanced, and the firm liked things to balance. Why would they pay for more spaces than they needed? Customers could park out front.

Pulling the briefcase out of the SUV, she walked to

the high rise. The elevator was opening, and she stepped in, unfolding the hometown newspaper. High heels or not, she was still a hometown girl. She considered herself one of the "lake people" like her parents. She worked in the big city for the money, but her soul was at the lake. The front page of the thin weekly rag showed a boat upside down and a headline that read: "Local Man Drowns in Boating Accident." She read the name of the victim, and her heart stuck in her throat. Jeff Larson was Chris' uncle—and that meant Chris would be in town for the funeral. Her heart desperately wanted to see Chris—and her head knew it was a bad idea. However, that hadn't stopped her before.

She loved Jeff and his family and knew Jeff's sister, Maggie, would be devastated. She needed to at least send a card or flowers. Maybe go by the house? She kicked herself for even thinking of that. She wanted to see Chris. He would be the draw. But she did care about the family. She'd known them for a long time. At one time, she thought she might become a part of that family. Maybe it would be best to stay away and not cause a scene. Just a simple card, she thought to herself as the elevator opened and she walked down the hall to her office where a load of work waited on her.

Chapter 6

Maggie and Jeff grew up on the lake and knew the best land and the best views. Their childhood had been dysfunctional at best, but they held each other up when things were tough. They spent many days on the lake just to get away from home. Their father was a dictator, and their mother was unable to stop him when he was on a tirade.

When Maggie married Paul, they bought the wooded lot that became their home because she said the lake soothed her soul. Even before they built, she loved to sit for hours watching the shore birds, geese, and occasional deer in the forest. They soon built their home from plans they had stored in a cedar chest at the end of their bed and began to live on the lake she loved. Their children were born and raised here and came home frequently. She thought they loved it too.

It didn't take long after her marriage for her brother, Jeff, to find someone to live his life with. It was obvious they were immensely happy, and Maggie was thrilled. Maggie remembered the first time she saw Cher. She sat on the park bench wearing a floral sundress, her blonde hair blowing in the breeze. The antique amethyst ring on the middle finger of her right hand sparkled in the sun as she spun it around. It was a gift from an old lover and was her favorite—the ring, not the lover.

Then the unthinkable happened. Cher was killed in

an auto accident. She was still wearing the amethyst ring on one hand and her wedding ring on the other the day the semi broadsided her compact car. Her death was instantaneous, thankfully.

The death of Jeff's wife had left him reeling, and he spiraled into depression and alcohol. It was Paul's suggestion that Jeff moved in with Maggie and Paul. It wouldn't be forever, but until he got his feet on the ground. But years later, even after their children were born, he remained. And it seemed normal to have him in the house. He was part of the family.

When Jeff moved in, he said it would be temporary, but the years went by, and the temporary became the permanent. Jeff was a wonderful uncle to her kids and treated them as his own. They loved him and were used to him being in the house especially when their father, Paul, was away on business. He was like a second father and, even when drunk, he never mistreated them.

Jeff stayed with Maggie and Paul even after his drinking increased. But Paul never said anything derogatory about Jeff. After all Jeff was her brother and Paul loved him too and allowed him to stay because he knew how much it meant to Maggie.

When the funeral home gave the family Cher's effects, the ring was in a tiny velvet bag along with her wedding ring. Jeff couldn't deal with even touching the bag or anything else that belonged to Cher. Maggie cleaned out the rented house of all Cher's belongings. She smelled her scent on the clothes as she cleared the closet and ached for her sister-in-law. She was more than her sister-in-law, she was her friend, and she felt she was betraying her by throwing all evidence of her life into trash bags and carting them away.

But Jeff didn't need to wake up the next day to her house shoes by the bed or her sweaters in the closet. He told Maggie to just get rid of it all. She did, except for the rings. They were still in Maggie's jewelry box along with her mother's. Maggie's things were delegated to a small box on the dresser.

Maggie moved to the bedroom in her own house that had always been Jeff's. Now she would clean out Jeff's things from the house, again like she had Cher's and her mother's, disposing of all evidence of a loved one's life.

Her brother had always been her best friend. Even with his drinking after his wife died, he was still her best friend and a part of her family. She couldn't believe that he just fell out of the boat. It wasn't like him, drunk or not. He knew boating safety and respected a large body of water.

Maybe Jeff didn't just fall out of his own boat and drown. There was something happening on Keystone Lake. Lake levels too high, fish disappearing, and landowners up and moving away almost overnight. Too many people were talking about it.

Chapter 7

The last customer of the evening finally left Buddy Mac's Bait and Tackle shop. It had been a long day. The owner locked the door and began to count the money in the register. It wouldn't take long—hardly anyone came in anymore. It was hard to make a living selling worms and plastic bait, so he had added beer and cigarettes a few years ago. Then came the sandwiches and chips, and soon he had a convenience store with a bait shop on the side. But everyone still called it Buddy Mac's Bait and Tackle. Boaters needed more than bait, and it would take more than bait to keep the doors open. The dock sat off one end of the store and had a place to tie up a boat with a small parking lot out back for road traffic. The bank would like it just fine if he kept the doors open and the mortgage paid. There were others, though, who would just as soon he went out of business; people who wanted his prime lake-front property for their own.

Many of his neighbors had left the lake due to the flooding this spring. At least he thought that was why they left. Some just disappeared without a word. Life was like that sometimes.

Looking out the window he stared at his lake which sat much closer to the store than in times past. The sun set about half an hour earlier giving it a beautiful golden glow. Money or no money, Buddy Mac loved this lake. It had always been his home and hopefully would remain so. The lightning in the distance caught his eye. There wasn't supposed to be any weather in the forecast, but it had been a wet spring.

He locked the front door and flipped the "open" sign to "closed." Picking up the bank-bag and grabbing his keys off the hook, he headed for the dock. He always made one last check around before going home for the night. Walking to the end of the dock, he saw the stringer of fish still hanging on the nail. He told Harry not to leave his fish there overnight. He could hang them on the dock long enough to get his stuff in the pickup, but he had to come back and get them. It was a waste of good fish to just leave them there to die. Besides, there didn't seem to be as many fish in the lake as there once was. He thought that had something to do with the chemicals dumped into the water to kill off the zebra mussels. It hadn't done the environment any good, but he guessed it was a trade-off. The dam was in trouble and had to be taken care of.

He pulled up the stringer and stared at the fish. Some of them were still alive. He carefully unhooked each one dropping them gently back into the water. That way they at least had a chance. He knew some of them would be washing up on the shore tomorrow.

Standing and turning around he picked up the bank-bag and walked to his car parked under a tree in the dark. He left the good parking places for customers and always parked in the back of the building.

As he reached for the door handle, the shovel hit him in the back of the head before he could react.

****

Buddy Mac fell face forward into the dirt dropping the money. Decker reached down and pulled his lifeless body to the rear of the car parked in the dark. It wasn't easy. The man weighed more than he appeared to when Decker first saw him. Decker hoisted him up and dumped him unceremoniously into the trunk. He picked up the man's keys and the bank-bag. It would be a bonus. Who couldn't use a little extra cash?

Decker didn't plan to have to kill for his new boss, but he promised it would only be the one time—and someone no one would miss. It ended up being more than once. And someone missed that Larson guy. He was all the talk in the tiny town of Mannford. But he didn't have to worry about that at the moment. He was a drunk, and everyone thought he just fell out of the boat and drowned. Maybe he did.

Now to make sure that Buddy Mac's body would not be found. He started the old man's car and drove off down the road. There was a place he knew of by the lake that very few people frequented. He'd have to walk a little way, but his pickup was parked not too far away from where he would push the car into the lake. He needed the exercise anyway. His nighttime job was sedentary, and he was getting flabby.

Chapter 8

Maggie's children were her world. Her son, Chris, a nature photographer, was often in remote areas, so she didn't see him as much as she wanted. But she loved him dearly.

He always tended to lean more toward his father than her. She guessed that was how it was with boys, they emulated their fathers and uncles more than their mothers, but she sometimes was jealous of their relationship. It was a world in which she was not an equal. She couldn't imagine how he would take the news of his uncle's death. Jeff was always a big part of the children's life.

Her daughter, Hope, on the other hand, could talk and shop for hours with her mother. They didn't always agree, but they found mutual ground on which to communicate. She was a devoted mother of five, two sets of twins and an extra, and had a seemingly great marriage. The house, the kids, even the dog seemed perfect. Hope was a marvel. The fifth child, even though unplanned, was as well-adjusted as the first, and each was an individual.

Maggie fingered the photograph of Hope's family. The children inherited their father's good looks and blue eyes. They would be tall like him. Her grandchildren were little stair-steps, and Maggie sometimes wondered if Hope felt like a baby factory shelling out one after another. However, Maggie was sure the children didn't feel like they were manufactured on an assembly line. They each appeared to be certain of their place in the family. All of them loved to come to Grandma's place at the lake and play on the beach or go out on the boat. Maggie taught each of them to swim in the cove she looked at every day. Maybe next year she'd teach the baby.

She instinctively knew she would feel better as soon as Hope arrived. Hope would take charge and make things work. Maggie never thought she was good at making plans come out right. No matter what she did, it was never as good as she wanted it to be. The roast was dry, the second layer on the cake slid sideways, the flower garden never bloomed at the right time, or her job at the university was always on the verge of something. Hope would be able to do a better job than her of making Jeff's funeral something he would have liked.

"I said, do you know what that message on the recorder was about?" asked Allison. The sound of her voice brought Maggie back to reality. Maggie still retained the old land line in addition to her cell phone mostly for Jeff. He liked the phone in the kitchen, and he could handle the technology of buttons on a recorder. So could his fishing buddies.

"What message?" she asked.

"You know, the one you said you didn't recognize. The voice that just said, 'Nine o'clock northwest corner of dam,' the one we were just talking about. Do you think we should mention it to the sheriff?"

"It was probably one of the guys talking about where to meet to fish last night. Erase it if you want." It seemed unimportant to Maggie who was trying to decide between the brown or blue suit for Jeff. She always hated details like that, mostly because she knew she would later regret her choice for one reason or another. The brown was too dark, or the blue didn't go with the tie. She was always second guessing herself.

They both looked out the window when the minivan pulled in. The noise was about to begin. The sound of children laughing would be music to her ears, and Maggie needed music right now. She expected to see the herd of kids come tumbling out. Instead, it was only Hope in pale yellow Capri's and matching blouse. Her hair and makeup were perfect even though Maggie knew she never spent much time on them. She was a natural beauty but seemed unaware of it. She just had to take care of herself in a hurry, she always said, because someone always needed some portion of her time.

Hope hugged her mother tightly. Maggie never wanted to let go, but when she finally did, they were both crying.

Maggie looked back at the van. "Where are the kids?"

"The neighbor came by and said she'd stay with them tonight. She knew I'd want to be with you right now." Hope sniffed and wiped her nose. "I can't believe he's gone. He was going to take all the kids fishing this Sunday. Do they know what happened yet?" she asked.

"Just that he drowned. I think he'd been drinking, maybe he fell asleep and fell out of the boat. I think they're going to just rule it an accident. But I'm not sure." Maggie poured a cup of tea for her daughter.

Hope arched one eyebrow as she took the teacup from her mother. "But he was always safety conscious in the boat, at least with the kids. What was he thinking?"

"The sheriff brought his things by while you were in the shower," Allison said. "I put them in the utility room on top of the dryer. They're in a sack. I didn't know if you wanted to go through them or not."

Maggie shook her head. "I don't know. Maybe later," then paused. "Something about this is not right. But I don't want to look at them right now. I'll look at them later. We need to go to the funeral home to make arrangements, eventually." In spite of herself, Maggie sat down with the tea pot in front of her and scratched her head. She looked at her daughter and friend who came rushing to her aid as soon as they heard. Like they didn't have lives of their own. But first tea. There would be time enough for the funeral home after tea.

Hope looked over the top of her cup blowing gently to cool it. "Oh, Chris called me back. He got the message and said he would get the first flight out and be here late tonight."

Maggie remembered their tea parties when she was a little girl. Time passed so fast.

"How did he take it?" Maggie asked.

Hope took a sip and then stirred a scant spoonful of sugar into the cup. "Actually, better than I thought he would. He sounded like he expected it or something. He was sad, but not surprised."

"That sounds strange—I mean like he expected it."

"Maybe not that he expected it, it was just that he'd talked to Uncle Jeff lately and knew he was upset over something," Hope said.

Maggie once more looked into the distance. "I'll be glad when he gets here. I'll feel better when the whole family is here."

As if on cue, Maggie heard tires on the gravel

driveway and glanced back out the kitchen window. Paul was home. She'd called him, and he said he'd leave right away. Away on business, it took a while to get back. He flew in and out of Tulsa and left his car parked at the airport. But he was finally home.

Now if Chris were home, the family would be complete.

Chapter 9

Maggie woke hearing Chris' voice and instantly sat up reaching for her robe, tiptoeing to the kitchen careful not to disturb Paul.

"I thought they might do a little more investigating, rather than just ruling it an accident," Chris was saying. "Everyone evidently assumes he was drunk and fell overboard."

"Like it or not, I think that's exactly what happened." Hope stood in the kitchen with her brother. It was the house they grew up in, and where now as adults they drank their morning coffee.

Her adult children still felt at home. Maggie smiled.

"I thought he was making a little headway with the drinking. At least that's what he told me the last time we talked. He said he had to keep his head together." Chris took a long drag on the coffee that had finally become the right temperature for drinking.

"...head together for what?" Maggie stood in the doorway in her robe and slippers watching the children she raised from infants.

"Mom, I didn't know you were up, did we wake you?" Walking to her, Chris hugged his mother.

"Actually, I don't remember going to sleep." Maggie pulled her robe around her. "When did I go to bed? And what time did you get in?" She hugged her only son again. He was never home enough.

"I got in around midnight, and everyone was already asleep. I crashed on the couch."

Hope smiled at her brother. "I found him in the kitchen when I got up. I don't think he sleeps much anymore."

"I'm not used to mattresses much these days. I don't feel right unless there is a rock under my sleeping bag, I guess. How are you doing? Hope says you sleep like the dead." Chris eyed his mother intently.

Maggie shrugged, then smiled. "I'm so glad to see you, you look well. I guess Hope told you we are having the service on Monday. As usual, your sister came to the rescue and planned everything." Maggie nodded to her daughter.

Chris nudged his sister standing next to Mom. "She always makes the details work out. I talked to Dad this week. He was telling me he and Uncle Jeff had a meeting with the Corps of Engineers coming up. Something about the dam. He said they weren't letting the water out fast enough after all the rain you've had lately, and he wanted to give someone a piece of his mind. The lake has been really flooded lately, hasn't it?"

Maggie nodded. That had certainly been on Jeff's mind lately. The flooding disrupted the fishing. At least that is what she thought he said. It's funny that you realized just how little you listened to a person until after they are gone. She couldn't remember how much she studied his face lately, had she really looked at him recently? Was he that worried about the dam?

Sleepily, Paul walked in wearing pajamas. "Chris!" He reached past Maggie and hugged his son. "I must have slept through you coming home. It's good to see you, son."

"You too, Dad," Chris said hugging his father.

"I'll fix some breakfast." Maggie reached for the skillet and opened the refrigerator to see what was inside.

"None for me, Mom. I don't normally eat breakfast, any more than sleep in a decent bed. But can I take the boat out for a spin?"

"Sure," Paul said reaching for the coffee pot.

"Of course," Maggie said. "Just be careful. The lake is starting to recede leaving lots of limbs and debris behind. With all the flooding lately, one day, I had to take the backroads just to get out of here and on the road to Tulsa for work."

Paul took his first sip. "I don't know how much gas it has. It hasn't been used much lately."

"Be careful," Maggie called again as he walked out the door. Hope and Chris both knew the lake intimately, and Maggie was sure Chris would be careful, but being a mother was a hard habit to break.

"He still can't sit still," Paul said as he took another drink.

Chapter 10

As he navigated the waters through the logs and branches, Chris kept wondering how his uncle was able to see all the debris after dark. Mom said he went out during daylight, but had he been out in the cove after dark? He was found in the narrow stretch of water down from the beach where they grew up as children. As the water receded, the beach was becoming more visible even though it was still covered with limbs.

Chris graduated high school with a boy who became the deputy sheriff. But they weren't kids anymore and, when he called to ask about his uncle's death, Deputy Sheriff Eric Black was reluctant to give many details. There was little to tell. After much prodding, the deputy finally told Chris the exact location where they found Jeff and his boat. That was the destination Chris had in mind when he borrowed his parents' boat.

Chris made his way to the place where his uncle's body was discovered, his mind continued to ask why Uncle Jeff would take the little boat this far out when he had the ski rig available. Sometimes fishermen trolled close to shore and dead branches looking for fish. Maybe he just went out too far. Was he trying not to be seen by keeping close to the shore? Jeff was agitated the last time Chris talked to him but didn't say why. Chris's uncle often had a bad attitude, and maybe that was all that there was to Jeff's manner. Chris had asked his uncle if he was okay, but all he said was, "As okay as they'll let me be." It was a statement Jeff often used, meaning that the world wouldn't always let him do as he wanted to do.

Chris ran the boat up on the sand, raising the motor as the water became shallow, and jumped out tying the boat to a fallen tree. There were tire tracks, probably from the ambulance that transported the body. There was evidence of a campfire back in the trees that probably belonged to the camper who found his uncle. How did the camper find Jeff? Was he going for a swim in the dark? Most campers stuck close to the fire after dark. Maybe he needed to relieve himself and didn't want to go to the park bathhouse up the road. He wondered if he still needed a bathroom after running into a dead body on the beach or if nature took care of that for him.

After looking over the beach, he returned to the boat and headed to the area where they found his uncle's skiff. There were lots of branches in the water and lots of things under the boat scraping and scratching the bottom as he traveled slowly. Eric said they used the Lake Patrol's watercraft to pull the little aluminum boat out of the debris with a rope, then towed it onto the beach. Chris assumed it was still in the sheriff's custody because they hadn't returned it to his parents' house. He would ask Eric tomorrow. He wasn't sure why he wanted to see it; he just did. After all, his uncle was in it when he died, wasn't he?

He turned the boat toward the dam making a mental note to ask the deputy about the smaller boat when he got back to shore. He was sure they still had all the evidence locked away somewhere at the sheriff's office. He would ask to see what his uncle had in the boat with him. Of course, if the boat capsized, there would have been nothing in it. Did the Sheriff say that the boat capsized, or did his uncle just fall out? He wasn't sure anyone said exactly what had happened. The body was found in one place, and the little boat in another. It was, after all, a straightforward accident. His uncle had drank too much, passed out, and fallen overboard.

Somehow it seemed all too easy.

The last time he talked to his uncle, he went on and on about the Corps of Engineers ruining his lake. The water was too high, or too low, the fish were not biting—or did he say they were not out there anymore. Chris really wasn't listening. He was thinking about all the shots he still had to do before he could come back; shots that were still waiting on him to return. He didn't really mean the fish weren't out there anymore did he, just not biting. Chris thought his uncle needed some new tackle or maybe just a new location on the lake to fish.

Chris's father taught him to fish and enjoy nature. Chris took all he learned from his dad and added to it his love of photography and made it into a great paying career. He loved his work, almost as much as his dad had loved to fish. Chris and his dad became very close over the years. Even more so after he became an adult, a fact that seemed to bother his sister.

Chris knew Hope loved her father, but as a girl, she didn't like to do all the things fathers and sons did. Her father taught her to love the lake, but she was more likely to sunbathe on the front of the boat than fish off the back. Paul had often chastised Hope for not being involved in the thrill of catching the big one. But Chris wondered if Hope was aware just how proud Paul was of his only daughter and how thrilled he was with all the grandchildren she brought into his life.

He checked the fuel gauge. It was time to go back to the dock. The trip to the dam would have to wait until tomorrow and a full tank of gas. He headed back to his parents' dock where the boat sat most of the time.

"Good morning, Paul." Chris looked up to see an old neighbor at the dock. Allen White was their neighbor and friend for twenty years at least. "Chris, I'm sorry, you looked just like your dad for a minute there. I must be getting senile."

"Good morning, Allen, how have you been?" Chris tied off the boat and shook the hand of the older man.

"I'm the same as always, just older. I wanted to bring something by to let your family know I'm thinking of them with the death of your uncle. But you know since my wife died, I just can't seem to cook anything. Not that I ever could, but anyway, that's my excuse. How's your mom holding up? This has got to be really hard on her." Allen stood on the dock with fishing tackle in hand.

"I think she's okay." Chris climbed out of the boat and onto the dock.

"She's a strong woman. It was a great shock to all of us though. Your Uncle Jeff was still a young man." Allen leaned over to help Chris tie up the back end of the boat.

"Yes, he was."

"Did Paul and Jeff ever talk to that guy from the Corps? They was sure riled up about that. Jeff and me went out fishing the other night, and it was all he could talk about."

"What guy? Uncle Jeff mentioned that the Corps didn't seem to be looking after the lake to his satisfaction." Chris finished the knot and stood shoving his hat back on his head.

"Well, I'm not sure if I remember the name, he was from the Corps, and Jeff said he was going to give him a piece of his mind. I think they was going to meet at the dam one night this week or next." He paused looking out at the lake. "I guess your mom and sister have the funeral all together, I plan to be there. Seems like all I do these days is go from the doctor to the funeral home and back. But I plan on paying my respects to your mom and dad." Allen wiped the sweat from his aging brow.

"Of course, Allen, I'll see you at the funeral. You take care now and, if you think of that guy's name from the Corps, would you let me know? I'd really like to see if Dad or Uncle Jeff talked to him." Chris waved as he walked away toward his mother's house.

"You bet, Chris, see you later." Allen ambled toward his truck.

Chris heard him grumbling under his breath about being old and senile as he walked away.

Chapter 11

Maggie had wondered how she would ever survive this day. The very thought of placing Jeff's body in the ground, even though she knew his spirit was no longer there, was physically painful. She would never see Jeff again.

She wore the navy-blue suit with her mother's pearls. Paul, Hope, and Chris were at her side, and everyone made it through the service without any glitches. The church insisted on providing dinner for the family at the house after the service, and masses of friends and family came by Maggie's home to pay their respects.

Maggie sat by the fireplace in the old chair that had been her mother's. Every chair in the house was brought into the living and dining room area, and still there were people standing. There were people in the kitchen too, hanging around the large coffee urn that the church brought over. It was as if they were waiting on one last drip to fill their cup.

A tall young woman wearing a business suit entered from the kitchen. Her dark hair swayed from side to side as she glanced around. She seemed familiar as she continued into the living room, but Maggie didn't recognize her until the girl finally spotted her and smiled.

"Erin!" Maggie leapt from her chair and walked toward the woman in the gray suit. Pulling her into a familiar embrace, she stepped back and peered at her at arms-length.

"It's been so long since I saw you! You look wonderful. I hear you're a lawyer now."

"Yes, I'm living in Tulsa. I heard the news and had to come by. I'm sorry I missed the funeral. My mom sends her sympathy, too. She couldn't get away from work."

Maggie gestured for Hope to join them. The women instantly recognized each other. Hope held out a hand to the newcomer then sat next her mother. "Erin, it's so good to see you. I don't know that I'd recognize you if Mom hadn't pointed you out. How are you? It's been a while."

"It has been some time, Hope. It's good to see you, too. I just wish it had been under better circumstances. I'm so sorry about your Uncle Jeff." Erin crossed her legs and smoothed her skirt then looked around the room. "Did Chris make it back? I know he's all over the world these days. It's been ages since I've seen him."

"He's here somewhere. Probably out back with the guys," Hope said glancing behind her. She stood and looked down at her mother. "Tea? Erin, would you like some chamomile tea? Mom and I are big fans of the stuff."

Erin shook her head. "No thanks, I'm fine."

Hope disappeared into the kitchen and was back quickly with cups for both, handing one to her mother. She glanced uncomfortably in the direction of a strident voice.

"I can't believe he just fell out and drowned. He'd been a fisherman for a long time and knew the lake well. It just doesn't seem right." Patti stood eating one of the muffins she was famous for.

"I guess it just goes to show, you never know when your time is up. It could be one of us tomorrow," said an equally loud voice.

Erin looked behind her. Conversations like this were all around them. She readjusted in her seat, cleared her throat, and patted Maggie's arm. "I'm so sorry, Maggie. You know they mean no harm. People just don't think about what they say sometimes."

"You're right. But it is hard not to ask that question."

"But he did just fall out of the boat and drown, right?" Erin looked directly at Maggie.

"As far as we know," Maggie responded and took a sip of tea, then sighed. "Do you think all these people will stay much longer? I'm sure they mean well, but I could really use some rest."

"Probably not much longer. Perhaps if we don't offer them tea." Hope giggled, which made Maggie laugh. She wasn't sure why it was so funny, but the laughter felt wonderful. Hope always knew how to cheer her up, or maybe it was the tea.

Erin stood and looked at her childhood friends. "It was great to see you both. We should get together more often and under better circumstances." She nodded to the women and left the room heading back through the kitchen. Stepping onto the deck, she spied Chris talking to an older man.

****

Chris leaned against the railing on the deck at the back of the house. It was too crowded in there, and the men seemed to be congregating out back. His dad, Paul, talked to their neighbor, Allen, and Chris joined in the conversation.

"I think his name was Rogers or something. Can't remember the first name right now, but I believe his last name was Rogers. You know, Chris, getting old is no fun. Just when you think you feel like doing something you did a few years ago, your body or mind has a different idea. Just like not being able to remember a simple name."

"Chris." Erin walked toward the young man in a suit. She held out her arms hoping he remembered her from school. They had been classmates years earlier even though Erin was a year younger.

"Erin Sampson! I can't believe it. You grew up. You used to be that irritating little kid who came swimming in our cove sometimes." Chris hugged her.

"Well, I didn't know I was irritating." Erin pretended to pout.

"I was kidding. You are welcome here anytime." He smiled and blushed lightly.

"I just saw your mother, and I wanted to come by and pay my respects to your family about your uncle's death. It was so untimely. I'm really very sorry." The wind blew hair in Erin's face.

"Erin, this is Allen White, our long-time neighbor. Allen taught me to fish. And you remember my dad?"

"Paul, yes of course. I'm so sorry for your loss."

Paul nodded.

Erin reached for the older man's hand shaking it. "Pleased to meet you, sir."

He took her hand warmly. "Chris' dad taught him to fish. I just gave him the finer points. My wife and I couldn't have children, and we kinda adopted Chris. We always thought Chris hung the moon."

Erin glanced quickly at Chris then back to Allen. "And you were right," she said. "Again, I'm so sorry about Uncle Jeff. I'll get out of the way so others can come by. It was good to see all of you again." She walked away toward her car. The lane had become a parking lot with all the cars parked there today.

****

Sheriff Montgomery and his deputy, like everyone else in the tiny town, appeared at the house after the service to say how sorry they were about Jeff. But when they left it seemed like the cue others were waiting for, and the room started to clear out. Maggie was happy to see them go.

Allison and Hope picked up plates and cups and cleared the dishes. It was the sign, and the room began to clear. More people came by to shake Maggie's hand, hug her, and wish her well. She was amazed at how many friends they had. It wasn't often that they were all in the same place at the same time. She always felt that the good in people came out at the really bad times.

And she was equally glad to see them all go.

"I'm going to go change out of this suit," she said. "I'll help you with the dishes when I get back."

"Too late, already done." Hope came out of the kitchen drying her hands on a towel and putting on her shoes as she went. "I'm going to get the kids, and I'll be back in a little bit. I'm sure the neighbor is ready to have her life back. The kids want to go to the beach with Grandma and Papa." Maggie smiled for maybe the first time all day at the thought of her grandchildren.

"Good," Maggie said. "Pack them up, and we'll spend a few days together. Bring Ted too if he can get away. It will be nice to have the house filled with family again. I'll get the beds made up, and we can have a camp-out in the living room, just like old times." As kids, Chris and Hope always loved camping out in the living room, and so did the grandchildren. "And maybe we'll bake some cookies too. I know they need some sugar."

"Okay. I'll see what Ted's schedule is like, and we'll be back soon. Do you need anything while I'm out?"

"We might need some milk, but just hurry back with my grandchildren." Maggie smiled at her daughter knowing the grandkids would be just what she needed to keep her smiling.

Chris came out of the bedroom in his shorts and tee shirt looking more comfortable than he had in his suit. Maggie always thought he looked dignified in a suit, but he looked more like himself in his shorts.

"Dad, Allen, and I are going to the dam. I want to look at some things. We'll be back later. I have my cell phone if you need me." He quickly kissed his mother goodbye and left before there was time for questions. Typical Chris, she thought, always on the run, couldn't sit still for a minute. She was sometimes jealous of his energy, but always jealous of his time. Mothers and sons; there's was a different type of relationship, more assumed than verbalized.

Once in the kitchen, Maggie pulled out ingredients to make cookie dough for the grandchildren. They didn't have much patience with the actual making of the dough, but they loved to put it on the cookie sheet by the spoonful. They watched anxiously as they baked. Later she would read them a story she had written just for them, about their adventures in the kitchen. It was a book she had thought about for a long time but just recently put on paper. She thought they would love it, and she was right. They always asked Grandma to read their special book to them before bedtime.

When Hope came back with the children, Maggie made them all sandwiches from the leftovers of the church's dinner. Baby Sarah had her own food from a jar, and then they clambered around her to bake cookies. Each one took a turn on the stool and dropped the dough by various sizes onto the cookie sheet. Tiny bits to giant globs of dough made various sized cookies. Maggie watched being certain the tiny ones didn't burn before the bigger ones were done, but Grandma let each one create their own cookies. Their presence was like therapy in a bottle to Maggie, and she drank it down like an addict.

Due to their hard work, they all had cookies and milk before bedtime. Hope drew their baths, and afterward they lay down on the pallets in the living room floor for Grandma's bedtime story. Even Baby Sarah, with her bottle in her mouth, lay perfectly still and quiet while Maggie read the book to them. They listened intently until their eyes could not stay open and they succumbed to sleep.

When Maggie finished reading, there were sleepy smiles all around. Baby Sarah was already asleep with her bottle falling out of her pink and perfect mouth. Jenny and Jill were curled up holding their dolls close, and even Eric and Emory were quiet, which was unusual for the four-year-old twins.

"Okay," said Hope quietly. "Everyone get a good night's sleep, and in the morning we'll make pancakes for breakfast." She kissed each one and pulled their covers up to their necks.

Maggie smiled at the lights of her life. They had

been replacements for the kids Jeff never had. Her heart ached wishing he were here to see this. But he wasn't, and he never would be again. If he had been, all five would have been in his lap at once—and he would have found room for each one. They would have listened to the story from their place in his lap and then climbed down and onto the pallets Mom and Grandma had laid out for them. Things were different now that he was gone and would never be the same again.

Maggie wondered how the children were told about their uncle's death. She was sure that Hope did her best to make the children understand and comfort them at the same time. It seemed she couldn't remember even telling her own children. She must have told them by phone, but she wasn't sure.

She thought about these things as she put on her nightgown and prepared for bed. Everyday things that seemed unimportant were the thread that held her fast.

Chapter 12

It seemed to Maggie she'd been asleep for hours when she woke to a dry throat. The clock said only 11:30. Her sleep schedules might never get back to normal. But she needed something to drink. She grabbed her robe from the foot of the bed as she headed for the kitchen—when she heard voices on the deck.

"You saw it too," he was saying. "The level was too high, and the gates were not open. Why is that? Do they shut down the gates at night? They were open today you said. That makes no sense, not when the rivers are still dumping water in faster than they are letting it out. If it continues it will be catastrophic for the fish and wildlife not to mention for the town economically. There are people who have put their lives into this place. Where are they now, and why are they not raising the roof over the flooding?" Chris spoke as Paul and Allen stood on the deck in the dark.

"Well, ol' Buddy Mac from down at the bait shop, he just up and left," said Allen. "Seems no one knew why, he just up and shut the doors one day and left. No one even saw him leave, it was like he was here one day and gone the next."

"Donovan at the grocery store said he might have gone to this brother's in Arizona. But no notice, just up and left. Same thing happened with Smitty at the mechanic shop. Just gone overnight. I heard that he left boats out in the yard not even worked on. People just had to come get them and haul them away. That's not like Smitty, he might not have had half a brain in some ways, but he was a damn fine mechanic and never left a project unfinished." Paul shifted to his other leg with his arms over his chest as he spoke.

"Do you think they left because of the damage from the flooding?" Chris spoke again. "It seems like they would have been angry about the way things were being handled instead of just leaving town. As I remember, Buddy Mac was always up for a fight whether it was justified or not."

"Yeah, it don't seem right somehow. Those boys at the Corps were always a little hard to talk to, especially since the new guy took over, but never like this." Allen looked out toward the dark lake.

"Did you ever think of his name?" Chris asked.

"The new guy in charge of the Corps here at the lake, Roger something, no Rogers, Don Rogers! There I did think of it. Guess I'm not as useless as I thought!" Allen sounded proud.

"You're not useless, Allen, never have been, just a little forgetful these days, and it's not your fault. Your brain is probably so full of facts there's just not enough room for all of it." Maggie, standing at the door to her kitchen in the worn bathrobe, could hear the smile in Chris' voice.

"That's real nice, Chris, but there's no fool like an old fool, I guess. But I did think of that Rogers fella's name for you, didn't I?"

"Yes, you did, Allen, yes you did. You know it is really late, and Mom would be mad that I kept you out this long, why don't I take you back to the house?"

"No, I've got my own pickup out in the drive, I'll be fine, I can drive myself home. It's just down the lane a bit. By the way, I've been meaning to ask you, did you ever ask the sheriff about your Uncle Jeff's effects? Did he bring them back to your mom?"

"No, but I'll find out in the morning. You be careful driving home in the dark now. You sure you'll be okay?" Chris sounded genuinely concerned for the welfare of the older man.

"I'll be fine, Chris, just fine. Let me know what you find out. Good night." Allen walked down the steps toward the beat-up old pickup in the driveway.

"Good night, Allen." She could hear Paul's voice on the deck too.

Chris walked through the kitchen door. "Mom!"

Paul stepped forward and hugged his wife. "Maggie, I didn't see you there. How long have you been there, did we wake you?"

"No, you didn't wake me. I just came in for a drink. That's when I heard voices. Was that Allen White? He's out late; I don't think he normally drives after dark, does he?"

"He promised he would be okay driving alone, and I decided I had to let him. He acts so depressed these days since his wife died. Do you think there is a little dementia going on there?" Chris reached into the fridge for a bottle of water.

"Seems like a little more all the time, I'm afraid. It is sad, especially for a mind that was as sharp as his was in his younger years. He is such a jewel. I don't know what your dad and I, and the community, would have done without him all these years. He is one in a million."

"I've been meaning to ask you, did the sheriff's

office bring by Uncle Jeff's effects, or do they still have them? I mean the things he had with him in the boat. Or was there anything in the boat—it capsized, right?"

"You know, Chris, I didn't ask as many questions as I should have maybe, but I'm not sure. I've been in a daze lately, but I do remember Allison saying that the sheriff brought by something, and it was in a sack out on the dryer. I never actually looked. Yes, the boat was capsized and found floating downstream upside down. So, I doubt that there was much found."

"Is it okay if I look in the bag?" Chris walked to the utility room.

"Of course, honey, look at anything you want for as long as you want. I need something to drink, how about you?" Maggie nodded to Paul.

"Just some water would be fine." Paul stood in the kitchen staring off into space.

Maggie sat down at the table with the water. A remarkable thing, bottled water, it made you forget there was a tap over the sink. You just opened the bottle and drank.

Chris emptied a sack on the table. Out fell Jeff's wallet, keys, change, and some gum still in the soggy wrapper. Maggie picked up the damp gum. Ever since Jeff quit smoking, he chewed gum. He would say he "really gave that gum fits" sometimes when he had a craving for cigarettes. She ran her hands over the smooth leather of his billfold, and it still felt slightly damp. There was about $40.00 in bills and various credit cards, library card, lifetime hunting and fishing cards, pictures of the nieces and nephews, a card from Buddy Mac's Bait and Tackle shop, and a real estate broker she had never heard of, T & H Realty. All of them water stained and curling.

"Who is T & H Realty?" Maggie asked no one in particular.

Chris shrugged. "Don't ask me. You live around here, not me."

"I know, but I've never heard of them, and it says Mannford. I wonder why Jeff would have their card."

"You know realtors, always trying to drum up business. Someone probably pushed it into his hand in town or at the dock or something."

"I guess. I just had never heard of it before. It didn't sound familiar." Maggie ran her fingers over the smooth leather of the wallet again, and thoughts of Jeff came flooding back. It seemed he always needed a new wallet; he was hard on them. He overfilled them, and they developed a constant curve from sitting on them in his back pocket. He hated breaking in a new one.

"I can't believe that's all there is." Chris sat looking at the pile of objects on the table.

Paul studied the wallet. "I'm sure the rest is on the bottom of the lake where the boat overturned. It's a miracle this stuff stayed in his pockets."

"I guess. I just hoped something would give me an answer to what happened to him," Chris said.

Maggie cleared her throat and then she spoke. "I keep thinking of how he must have felt as he drowned. For the first time in my life, I hope he was passed out and unaware of what was happening to him. I keep having this awful dream where I can't breathe, and I think I must be drowning. I know it is silly, just stress and such, but I felt wet seaweed around my mouth. I just hope it wasn't that awful for him."

"Just stress, as you say, can be a powerful thing, Mom. I think you promised Allison you would see the doctor after the funeral. You know he might be able to give you something to help you get through this."

"I don't want to be an invalid. I can do this on my own. I have you and your dad and sister; at least I want to try. Please let me try for a little while?" Maggie wiped away the tears that came too often lately.

"Okay, for a little while, then we try it my way. I have already lost an uncle and don't want to lose a parent." Chris reached across the table and patted her hand. "For now, why we don't call it a night and get some sleep. I saw the pallets in the living room, and I know the little ones will be up early and want to play."

"I'm sure you're right. We should all get some rest. I love you, son."

"Love you too, Mom." Chris leaned across the table and planted a kiss on the top of her head then walked off down the hall to his old room.

Chapter 13

Morning came early with bright sunshine and a mild breeze.

Maggie kept thinking of the line from the Robert Browning poem, *God's in his heaven and all's right with the world*—but of course it wasn't.

Hope made the children pancakes, true to her word, and of course they wanted to take Grandma swimming at the beach. Jenny and Jill came out in their swimsuits ready to go even though the straps were not fastened. Hope tried to explain to them that the beach was underwater but to no avail. So Hope and Maggie packed the kids up in Hope's van and took them to see the damage from the flood waters firsthand. They asked where the beach went, and Maggie tried her best to explain that it was still there, just covered with water. She knew it must be hard for them. First their uncle was gone, and now this. She tried to make sure they understood that the beach would come back as soon as the water went down, but the concept was too mature for such little minds to grasp. Jenny and Jill cried which made baby Sarah cry, and Eric and Emory whined to go play.

"I think we should go to the park, and then we can have a picnic if you want. What do you think?" Hope always thought of ways to help her children cope.

A rousing chorus of "Park, park, park!" came from

the backseat. Evidently, the beach was forgotten, and off they went on a new adventure.

Maggie was sure the park would not be underwater since it sat on a hill and hoped that the children would enjoy the nice weather and play on the equipment. The playground was deserted, and the kids had their pick of which toys to play on. Hope and Maggie guided them to what Chris always called the "baby section" with the smaller swings and a great sand pile. They could still use their sand toys even if they weren't on the beach. That part of the park had its own fence, so mothers could sit and watch their children without having to chase them all the time. Maggie liked that idea for little ones. When her kids were little, she had to constantly make sure they were right with her, especially Chris who loved to go exploring.

"Mom, do you think Uncle Jeff just fell out of the boat and drowned? I mean, do you think he was so drunk he didn't know he was falling out? I keep thinking about this, and it seems to me that if a person were sitting in a boat and passed out, they would fall backward into the boat, not out of the boat. Have you thought about that?" Hope sat on the park bench with her mother watching the children play.

"I've thought about the fact that I hoped he didn't suffer and wasn't frightened knowing he was drowning, but not how he fell out. What do you mean exactly? That he might have had help falling out of the boat? Who would do such a thing? Your uncle had no enemies. He was a bit of a hothead sometimes, but everyone knew he was a well-meaning person, don't you think?" Maggie's attention was pulled to the kids and laughed as the boys played tag with their younger sisters.

"Yes, but I just keep thinking about how easily everyone called it a fishing accident and never really investigated the fact that there might have been foul play. Chris keeps going to the dam with Allen White, and Dad and talks about the problems with the flooding and the dam. Uncle Jeff was really upset about the condition of the lake lately; do you think there is any correlation between the two? I mean Uncle Jeff's drowning and the fact that he was going to the dam to meet with the Corps that evening. And Dad was going with him, though I'm not sure he knew why. I think he was just following along for Uncle Jeff's sake."

"Your uncle was just fishing, Hope, not going to the dam."

"That's not what the message on the answering machine said." Hope would not be swayed.

"What message?" Maggie was hardly listening as she watched the children's antics.

"You know, the one that said, 'Nine o'clock, northwest corner of the dam' and nothing else. Allison said that you two discussed it. She said you just dismissed it as one of Uncle Jeff's fishing buddies, but she wondered if it was something else."

"You know Allison. She always reads things in where there is nothing. I don't remember discussing it with her, but there are a few gaps in my memory the last few days. I don't mean to be harsh about Allison, she is always there for me when I need her, but I really doubt if it meant anything. Who did she think it was on the tape?"

"I think that was the problem. She didn't know and thought maybe you would. Did you listen to the message?" Hope wiped a smudge off the baby's face.

"No, I don't think I did. Is it still on the tape or did we delete it?"

"I think it is still there; maybe you should listen to it when we get home. You would know better than anyone who the voice belongs to. Maybe I am just grasping at straws. I hate the idea that Uncle Jeff might have met someone out on the lake who would hurt him." Hope smiled at the baby, rocking her back and forth as she fussed.

It was nearly noon and Hope asked Maggie to keep an eye on the kids while she went to the van for the picnic basket. Sarah was getting cranky and wanted her bottle. Maggie knew if she got her bottle now, she would drink it down and go to sleep without lunch and would wake up hungry in an hour and still tired. So they decided to feed the children now and not wait. Hope returned with baloney sandwiches and milk for everyone. They also had cookies left over from last night for dessert. Sarah had her food in jars that her mother packed but was really eyeing the sandwiches everyone else was eating. It was hard being the baby and not being able to eat what the big kids ate. But eat she did, enough that her mother gave her a part of a cookie for a reward before her bottle. The cookie made her smile sleepily, and Hope knew the bottle would be the end of her. She would start her afternoon nap before they were home.

Chapter 14

Chris' cell said "Ryan." He never erased her from his contact list—even after all these years. They'd never called each other since the breakup. But he heard she worked in Tulsa now as accountant at a big firm. And he hadn't been able to quit thinking about her since the funeral when he saw her at a distance. He smiled remembering the times they went skinny dipping in the lake they grew up on.

"Ryan," he answered, still smiling.

"Hey, Chris." She still had the small-town-girl twang to her voice. Bet she didn't in the office. Bet she was all business there. "I called to say how sorry I was to hear about your Uncle Jeff. I know you two were real close."

"Thanks. News travels fast, even in Tulsa. I actually saw you at the funeral but didn't get a chance to say hi. I guess you're still in Tulsa?"

"Yeah, well I work in Tulsa. I live in Mannford."

"How many kids do you have now? Still married to what's-his-name?"

"His name was Kenny."

Chris looked out onto the lake, and images of Ryan's naked body in the moonlight made him smile again. Keep it together, bud, he thought to himself. Ryan was the only woman who ever affected him this way. And it was just as well. He needed to keep his head on straight and not be distracted. She could do that to him.

"Was?"

"Probably still is. We don't talk anymore—not since the divorce."

"Divorced, huh? Who saw that coming?"

"All right, I don't need a lecture from you. He was a mistake, but I was on the rebound. Anyway, no kids, which is for the best under the circumstances."

"I'm sorry. I know you wanted the husband, kids, and white-picket-fence thing." Chris walked down the dock toward his parents' boat. He wanted to spend as much time as possible out on the water while he was here.

"Yeah, well you know. I guess I got the husband-thing, and it wasn't all it was cracked up to be. You going to be in town long, or you off on another adventure?"

"I don't know how long I'll be here, just checking on some stuff for Mom and Dad. Want to meet up while I'm here?" He knew it was a long shot. When they broke up, it set her back really hard. What she didn't know was how badly he felt afterwards. He loved her, but he loved the job too, and she wasn't going to tag along with him and just sit around waiting for him to be finished. What woman would?

"Sure. Pick me up at the convenience store in town. I'll be waiting." She clicked off.

Did she mean now? He looked again at the boat and then out at the water. He untied the boat without thinking and climbed in. They'd met at the same convenience store the whole time they dated in high school and some even in college. He knew where she would be. The store backed up to the cove, and he could pull the boat up to the bank—if the waters weren't too high. Yes, he knew where she would be waiting.

He pushed the boat as fast as it would go across the water heading for the small town and the cove where they'd met a thousand times. What was he thinking getting involved with her again? It would only end poorly. As he slowed the boat down, rounding the corner, he saw trees in the water that used to be on the bank. The dock attached to the back of the store was nowhere to be seen. He put the boat in reverse, slowing the forward motion, and eventually backing it out of the cove. Was the dock still there just waiting to put a hole in Dad's boat, or had they removed it? And then he saw the post sticking out of the water. An inexperienced boater would have hit it. Instead, he backed out and came around to park on the side. The dark water smelled stagnant under the willow trees. Not good for wading. The lake was not the same as it had been when he'd lived here. Maybe it never would be again. He carefully backed out again and pulled to the front of the building where the weekenders parked their boats.

And there she stood.

Sun shone off auburn hair and tanned legs. She still wore the cut-off jeans she used to wear in high school. Not much had changed. Well, everything had changed, but she still looked as good as the day he left.

Tying the boat again, he climbed out walking her way. She smiled and ran to him giggling, throwing her arms around his neck. Her hair smelled like coconut as he buried his face in it. She stepped back just short of his kiss. Okay, maybe not everything was the same.

"It is so good to see you!" Ryan smiled radiantly in the sunshine. "I'm so sorry about your uncle though."

"Thank you." Chris still had his hand on her waist

unwilling to let go until she made the first move. "Are you not working today? It's the middle of the week."

"I had some vacation time and decided to use it." Her smile radiated in the sunlight, and as the old feelings surfaced Chris knew he could be in trouble.

On the other side of the boat dock an old man sat in an aging Chevy with the radio station cranked up so loud everyone in the parking lot could hear it.

"The Corps of Engineers are concerned about the zebra mussels populating waterways at an alarming rate. They can do irreparable damage if not stopped. Zebra mussels are freshwater mollusks invading lakes and rivers nationwide," the news announcer said.

"Old Charlie is still around." Ryan nodded to the Chevy. Chris turned to see the old man who seemed old even when they were kids.

"Yeah, some things never change." Chris looked back at the auburn hair that blew lightly in the breeze.

The radio continued to blare as the man snoozed in the afternoon sun. *"Their origins stem from the lakes of southern Russia, where they attached to tankers in the freshwater of the ballast and made their way into the Great Lakes, then down the Mississippi and her tributaries. Now they are everywhere, even clogging the mighty Hoover Dam and dams downstream in Lake Havasu and the Colorado River. These areas provide water and hydroelectric power for millions of people while the tiny parasite procreates with abandon. Divers are often contracted to use giant vacuums to remove them from the turbines of the dam where they can choke the workings and shut down the production of electricity."* The announcer droned on and on.

Chris moved away from the noisy radio. "But the

zebra mussels are causing trouble around here, too. They keep trying to get rid of them using chemicals like chlorine and sulfuric acid to kill them. You can imagine how the environmentalists feel about that." Chris guided Ryan toward his father's boat tied up at the dock.

"Boaters who travel from lake to lake are asked to thoroughly wash their boats, motors, and trailers before entering other lakes. The adult mussels have been known to live outside water for up to two days. If they are moved from one body of water to the next, they can set up residency anywhere. Therefore, they should be removed before entering a different body of water. Ongoing research is being done to provide a solution to the mounting problem." The radio suddenly changed to a popular musical number. Evidently, the news was over.

Chris smiled and moved Ryan farther away from the noise. "Wanna take a ride? When was the last time you were on this lake?" Chris smiled at the woman who used to sneak out of her bedroom window and meet him at the dock.

"It's been ages, and I'd love to," she replied, climbing in the boat.

Chris pulled away from the dock in his parents' boat feeling like a teenager again. Beside him was the woman he'd been in love with so long ago.

Maybe he still was.

Chapter 15

Finally, the lake levels did recede. The rains let up—at least for a while. Beck's Beach returned just as the warmth of spring hit its peak. And Maggie needed a swim. She walked the path to the beach in her swimsuit, flip flops, and a towel tied around her waist. She hung the towel on a piece of driftwood and kicked off her flip flops. Her body acclimated to the temperature changes by wading up to her knees at first. Splashing the water on her arms and neck, she watched a school of shad jumping in the sparkling water. A quick dive took her under, and she felt the cold water slide gently over her warm body. Swimming was the one thing in her life that never changed. It took over her body and left her mind to wander. She swam underwater as far as her breath would take her and then surfaced. She began a nice slow crawl stroke checking her distance from the shore now and then. She felt she had gone far enough when she reached the branch that stuck up in the water, then returned with a back stroke until her butt hit bottom. It was far enough. She sat up in chest deep water and leaned back to survey the lake, her home. She loved this lake more than anything except her family. This lake was her solace in good times and bad.

Lately enough bad had come into her life. First Jeff's death and now the real estate mess. Someone in her small well-loved town made a pact with the devil it seemed. Real estate prices were plummeting, and people were leaving in droves. It first started with small businesses going under, then weekend people sold out too. The rumor was that the local bank was calling in notes. For Sale signs littered the landscape, and foreclosures were frequent. Paul and Maggie's home was paid for, and they both had good jobs, Maggie thought they would be okay financially. But her friends and the town she loved were not faring so well.

Another few laps, and she would work on the rose garden. The roses were pruned in early March, but they needed to be fed, weeded, and some needed deadheading. The rose garden was something Maggie convinced Paul to help her put in when they were young. He thought roses would never grow in the rocky soil with all the shade around them, but Maggie disagreed. He said they lived despite the conditions because she willed them to. Maggie knew it took lot of work along with some willpower. Paul also helped her dig drainage for the bed so that it coincided with the natural lay of the land. However, lately some of the older bushes began to wither on the south side of the ditch. She thought maybe they were losing more water than the ones on the opposite side. She wished Jeff were around so she could bounce some ideas off him. He was a great gardener, and she always depended on his level head to help her with such problems. Maybe she should talk to someone at the local nursery about what was happening to her roses.

She stood up in knee deep water as the boat approached. It was Patti and Sam Smith and their familiar yellow Sea-Do boat. They worked in Tulsa during the week but came out to the lake on the weekends to play.

"Hi, neighbor. It's good to see you swimming again." Patti took off her sunglasses and placed them on top of the floppy hat that covered her head.

"It is great to be able to swim again. I was so tired of the lake levels so high you couldn't find the beach anymore, let alone use it for swimming. Catching any fish?" Maggie walked deeper into the water toward the boat.

"We were really just surveying the damage, not fishing. No one wants to try to fish anymore. It seems like the fish have just vanished anyway. I guess they are still in shock about the water levels." Sam idled the engine on the boat as he spoke, then shut it off.

"Maggie, I know we've said this before, but we are still so sad about Jeff. Did anyone ever decide just what happened?" Patti shaded her eyes with her hand.

"Thank you, but no, we just think he fell out of his boat." Maggie wondered how many times she had answered that same question.

"But that was so unlike him. He was such a safe boater." Patti shook her head.

"I know. But these things happen, I guess. Anyway, it was nice of you to ask. I was just about to go back to the house and do some gardening, enjoy your boat ride and be safe." Maggie stepped back toward shallow water.

"We will, and you and Paul please come up to the house some time, and Sam will grill some steaks. You know his steaks are the best on the lake!" Patti waved as Sam restarted the boat and slowly left the cove.

Maggie nodded and started toward the beach. She picked up her towel and flip flops on the way up, wrapped the towel around her waist, and slid her feet into the flip flops before walking back up the path to the house.

Pulling on the shorts and tee shirt over her wet suit, she found her pruners in the potting shed. The roses needed deadheading. Some were getting black spot even though they were well drained on the hill. Dusting them was the only way to get rid of it.

The day was warm, and Maggie's tee shirt, that had dried in the wind, was soon soaked again by perspiration when she was finished. She was dirty and sweaty but liked the way she felt physically, better than she'd felt in a long time. The exercise was a Godsend. She squatted down beside the roses and looked out onto the lake. Her lake. The day was hers, and for once she felt ready to face it. Already dirty, she would go for a hike. A shower could wait.

Her hiking boots were on the back porch with dirty socks still inside. Dried, caked mud flaked off as she pulled them on her feet. The last time she wore them they went hiking at the end of the old highway. Paul and Jeff liked to fish off the old broken highway sometimes. It was good habitat for fish. She sometimes went along for the walk. Catching something was gravy, they always said. Just fishing was enough.

The deep shade cooled the air at least ten degrees as she hiked the path to the lake. Flies buzzed around her at first, but the farther she walked the fewer the insects. Then at the edge of the bog, she realized just why she was there. This part of the lake was inaccessible by land a few weeks ago. When the level of the lake was higher, this was the area where they found Jeff's boat. She was unsure exactly where, but somewhere near the ancient oaks that lined the edge of the water. Jeff's boat was floating upside down, and they pulled it out of the vegetation with the patrol boat.

She worked her way around the muddier areas and observed the water mark on the trees. It was incredible to imagine the water was once this high. It must have been six feet in this area, over her head. She stumbled over a log, falling on her knees in the mud and smashing her hand into something hard. Pain radiated up her arm. Probably a beer bottle. Maggie knew the local kids partied here in good weather. The floods prevented them from having their festivities here lately.

Picking up her hand, she flipped it over expecting a severe cut. No blood dripped from a gash, just a deep crease that would probably bruise. At least she wasn't bleeding with nothing to stop it. This area was part of the algae bloom earlier in the season before the rains and flooding began, and she didn't need bacteria causing an infection.

Then she saw it.

The hard metal that contacted her bare hand was the lid to a commuter cup. It looked like the one her brother always took with him. The silver metal lid was caked with mud but still held tightly to the camo print plastic bottom, buried in silt. Maggie dug in the mud freeing the cup and thinking of her brother. The boat Jeff was in washed up here, but where did it capsize? His body was found elsewhere. She stared out into the water thinking of Jeff.

A blue heron nimbly fished in the distance in shallow water. No one around but Maggie to disturb him, and she was obviously no threat. He stood on one leg, toes poised and beak hovering over the water as the tiny fish swam oblivious of his intentions. Slowly lowering his beak, his head snapped back with a single silver fish protruding from both sides of his mouth. Water dripped down his blue-gray feathers as he lifted his head and swallowed the fish whole. It was quick and seamless—the way he approached life. He had to eat, and fish were his favorite food. Mastering the art of fishing was the difference between life and death—and he was a master. She could learn a lot from the bird.

She carried the commuter cup with her as she hiked back to the house. She'd put it with the rest of her brother's things and maybe look at it later. She was unsure why she kept it, but she couldn't just leave it to litter the lake. But for now, she needed to get home and shower.

****

On the dryer in the utility room lay more remnants of her brother's life. The brown paper bag from the Sheriff's office sat open. She placed the muddy commuter cup beside it. Chris's wallet, stuck hastily back into the sack after they looked through it, slid out at an angle. Maggie dumped the contents onto the white metal dryer she'd owned since the kids were little. It was really time to shop for a new washer/dryer set. The old one took too long to dry a load of clothes. But lately she had not been in a shopping mood.

The gum still in its wrapper lay hard and stiff. The leather wallet, now dried, was equally stiff. Keys rolled to the other side of the dryer, and she picked them up rolling them around in her hand. Chris never used them again after that fateful night in the boat. And now he never would.

Next to the sack lay the mini cassette tape probably left their by her friend, Allison. It was a dinosaur in most households, but Maggie had kept it for Chris. He lived in the past, and the cassette was just one more example of his personality. A single tear spilled over the top of her lashes. She wiped it away.

In the kitchen, she slid the cassette once more into the machine and pushed play.

"Nine o'clock, northwest corner of the dam," was all that was on the message.

She replayed the message and heard the same thing. Rewinding the tape, she found there were no other messages. Chris must have erased them. Paul and Maggie never touched the answering machine. They had voice mail on their cells and Chris took care of his own messages. Once more she hit play.

"Nine o'clock, northwest corner of the dam." That's all that was said, and she had no idea whose voice she listened to. The voice was not familiar. Whoever it was didn't sound like they were from the area. Maybe a back-east accent. Rubbing her arms, she realized the voice gave her goose bumps. Something wasn't right. She'd felt from the beginning that Jeff didn't just fall out of his boat and drown. Yes, he drank too much, and yes, he was alone. But Jeff knew the lake, boating, and fishing better than anyone. He would have been more careful. If he was capable.

Back at the dryer, she picked up the cup and unscrewed the cap. It was half full, and she quickly screwed the lid back on the putrid smelling liquid. Whatever he'd been drinking that night was not beer. It didn't smell like bourbon either—the only other thing he drank. But it had been at the bottom of the lake for a while in the heat so that could have changed the chemical makeup of what was in the cup. She started to pour it out when it occurred to her. What if it wasn't just bourbon? What if it was something else?

She put the tape and the commuter cup back in the sack. She had to have a shower, and then she'd take these to the sheriff's office and insist that they run tests on the liquid and listen to the tape.

What if her brother didn't just drown? What if he was murdered?

Chapter 16

Maggie stood at the desk of the local sheriff's office, brown paper bag in hand.

She plopped the bag on the desk. "Sheriff, this is the sack of things you brought to the house—Jeff's effects. My family and I went through them and found nothing unusual. However, I do have some things that might be." She pulled the cassette tape from the bag. "This tape is the one used in the recorder attached to our phone, and I thought you might want to listen to it. It says very little. It seems to be instructions from someone on when to meet."

Sheriff Montgomery shifted in his seat looking uncomfortable. "You know this case is closed, Maggie."

She still stood holding the tape out to him with one eyebrow arched.

The sheriff sighed and then took the tape from her hand. "But we can listen to it. I think we still have a tape player around here." He dug in a drawer and came up with a hand-held dictation machine. "This might work."

"I also have something else. When the lake water receded, I hiked down where you discovered the boat and I found this buried in mud. It is Jeff's commuter cup. He always carried it, and it must have fallen out of the boat. The lid was still on it. When I opened it, the liquid was still in there, and it smells really bad. Not like something Jeff would drink. I mean, Jeff was a drinker, but this doesn't smell like bourbon. He only drank beer and bourbon. He was a picky drunk. And I have had a bad feeling about his death from the beginning. He wouldn't get drunk and just fall out of his boat. He grew up around the water. And this isn't bourbon." Maggie felt as if a weight had been lifted off her shoulders when she finished what she had to say.

The sheriff looked her up and down. "You don't think it's possible for Jeff to pass out and drown? It happens all the time, Maggie."

"Not to Jeff. He respected the water, and he knew his limitations. I want you to have this liquid analyzed."

"Maggie, you don't know what you're asking. We're a small county and don't have the facilities for a lab."

"Send it to Tulsa. They have the facilities."

"We've already closed the case, and the cause of death was determined at the morgue."

"Did anyone check what was in his stomach, or did you just think the town was rid of another drunk?" Maggie felt her cheeks burn as her anger boiled up inside her.

"Now, Maggie, that is not what happened. We all cared about Jeff. But accidents do happen."

"Not this time. I have a feeling, and now I have some evidence. I need you to check on this." Maggie leaned on the desk closer to the sheriff.

"I can't spend county money on a hunch. I need more proof than that."

Maggie seethed. "Then listen to the tape. Who is that?" She pointed to the tape still in the sheriff's hand.

The sheriff grumbled something she couldn't make out and plopped the tape in the machine, rewinding it. He pressed the play button after cranking up the volume. It still worked after many years of lying in a drawer. "Nine o'clock, northwest corner of dam."

The sheriff's face contorted. "Nine o'clock, northwest corner of dam?"

Maggie cleared her throat. "Do you know that voice?"

The sheriff looked up. "I'm not sure. Maybe. But I can have it analyzed—and the contents of the cup. Can I keep this stuff?"

"That's why I brought it to you."

Chapter 17

The smell of burgers filled the air on Maggie's deck. Kids ran and squealed in the sweet light of evening. It would be a chore to get them to sit still and eat. But the main idea behind tonight was to get the family together and not think about Jeff's death. That could be for another day. And for once it wasn't raining.

Chris stepped from the house just as the music started—something he rigged up as a teenager that Maggie had forgotten about. Music was seldom listened to—and it should have been, she thought.

Chris grabbed Maggie's hand, smiling. "I'm surprised those old speakers still work." He danced his mother around the deck just as an SUV pulled up in the driveway. He stopped. "Um, I hope it's okay. I invited Ryan to have dinner with us."

Maggie's eyebrows raised. "Ryan? Your Ryan? I mean used to be. Of course, it's okay. I haven't seen her in years." Maggie watched as her son walked quickly to the car. Ryan stepped out with a bag in hand. She looked almost like the teenaged girl who used to hang out at her house when Chris was younger. Chris kissed her cheek and led her to the deck.

"Everyone, you remember Ryan," Chris' face changed to a light pink as he glanced around the deck at his family.

Hope held her hand out. "Ryan, so good to see you."

She beamed.

Hope waited as the children surrounded the beautiful redhead. Ryan spoke as each were introduced.

"Wow, you have such great kids." Then Ryan looked across the deck at Maggie. She walked toward her with her arms out. "Maggie, so good to see you. Thank you for allowing me to crash the party." She reached in the bag pulling out a large bowl of pasta salad. "I hope you like this. It is my aunt's recipe, and my family always loves it."

"Thank you! I'm sure it will be wonderful. I haven't seen you since—well, in a long time. I'm glad you came."

"Burgers are ready," Paul called from the grill and carried the first batch to the table. He stopped and stared. "Ryan, it's been a long time," he said and held out one arm for a quick hug.

The normal patio table served as the buffet, and Paul had pulled the folding banquet-length table from the garage. The family sat on chairs from the kitchen and the patio set. The children's table stood beside it and the baby, in Hope's lap, pulled to get down to join the bigger kids. She had her own food but sucked on macaroni from the salad Ryan brought.

The only sounds were the munching and giggles from the kids. Burgers were eaten, and even the mosquitoes stayed away leaving the family some much needed time together.

Fireflies could be seen blinking in the bushes in the distance as Paul flipped on the patio lights and Maggie lit the candles on the table. Baby Sarah lolled in her mother's arms. It was getting late, but no one wanted to leave.

The crunch of tires on gravel sounded as headlights shone on the deck from the compact car. Ted Shipley's long legs stepped out, and he unfolded, tossing something back inside.

"Family!" he shouted and walked toward the party climbing the steps.

Maggie thought she saw him stumble.

He stepped up, and kids swarmed him. He patted them each on the head. "Sorry, I'm late. Work, you know."

Maggie stood. "Ted, we saved you a plate. I'll warm your burger."

"No thanks. I've eaten."

He walked toward Hope and the sleeping baby reaching to take her. "She's sleeping, Ted. Let her stay here," Hope spoke quietly, and he sat down in the chair Paul offered.

Maggie smelled bourbon on his breath, and it reminded her of Jeff.

"Your meeting must have run long," Hope said quietly. "You should have called."

"Now, Hope, it's a beautiful evening, let's not ruin it." He smiled indulgently as Maggie handed him a glass of tea. He set it on the table.

"So, how is everyone. I'm not sure I know this lovely creature." He nodded toward Ryan.

Chris cleared his throat and eyed his brother-in-law. "Ted, you remember Ryan. We dated in school, and she was around before you and Hope were married."

Ted smiled. "Of course, it's been a long time. So, what's new?" He looked around at the people gathered in the evening air.

The deck was quiet. No one spoke, the air thick with

tension. Then Hope broke the silence as she stood. "We need to get the kids home. It's late. Sarah is already toast, and there are baths to take. I hate to be a party pooper, but the kids and I need to go home."

Maggie helped Hope gather up the children and all their toys and move the parade of tired kids to the van. "Mom, thanks so much. This was great."

"We need to do it more often." Maggie kissed her daughter's cheek.

Walking back to the house, she heard Ted ask Paul if there was anything stronger to drink than iced tea.

"I don't think there's been any alcohol in the house since Jeff died. Sorry, man."

Ted stood and stretched. "That's okay, I should probably help Hope with the kids. Thanks, and good night to everyone." He walked toward his car that sat next to where the van had been moments ago.

The people on the patio mostly sat in silence, and then Maggie began clearing what was left on the table. They all helped her take it inside.

Once inside Ryan helped put away the food. "I need to be going too. Thank you so much for allowing me to come." Ryan reached for her empty bowl on the countertop. "All gone. They must have like it."

"It was wonderful, and it was wonderful seeing you again," Maggie said, and Paul nodded.

Chris walked out the back door with Ryan. Maggie looked after them, silently wishing Chris and Ryan would get back together. She always thought she'd make a great daughter-in-law. Then she thought of Hope and wondered if her marriage was in trouble. The tension between the couple was obvious to anyone. She knew from experience what it was like to live with someone who drank to excess. She hoped this wasn’t a regular occurrence.

Chapter 18

Ryan walked back to her desk with copies of the deeds in hand—all made out to T & H Realty. Staring at the pile, she placed them in dated order. She couldn't believe the names on some of the deeds. People who had lived at the lake forever. People she knew.

She volunteered for the job in a meeting that day when it became obvious that real estate around her favorite lake was being snatched up for a song. She was curious enough about her hometown and the surrounding area to try to solve the mystery.

Erin Sampson, an attorney in Tulsa, was a girl Ryan had gone to school with back in the day. A little younger than Ryan, she still remembered her. But when the receptionist said an attorney from Cronkite and Associates was out front for her appointment, Ryan was surprised to see who it was. It was always easier to see the change in someone else rather than yourself. Ryan had changed too, she reminded herself.

A lot of water had gone under the bridge since high school. Ryan and Chris broke up in college, and then Ryan had made the biggest mistake of her life marrying Kenny not long after graduation. But what could you expect from a guy in a dirty pickup and an ever-present six-pack in the fridge? That wasn't really fair. There were a lot of good guys with dirty pickups, but Kenny wasn't one of them.

"Erin Sampson?" Ryan walked toward the girl she knew from school a long time ago .

Erin smiled. "Ryan. It's good to see you. I'm sorry I'm so late. Things kept getting in the way at the office. But I finally made it."

"No problem. And you! What have you been up to? I was told an attorney from Cronkite and Associates was here. And you're the attorney, wow! Life goes on and people change. Whatever happened to the little girl in the flower shop?" Ryan reached for Erin's arm guiding her to her office.

"Someone else took her job." Erin smiled. "I'm now with Cronkite and Associates, and we represent a homeowner's association that is concerned about the sale of property around Keystone Lake, mostly near the peninsula. They want to know what it is doing to their property values. Have you heard about it?"

"Actually, I've been putting together a spreadsheet with legal descriptions and property values—comparing the sales price and the appraised price. And there's a big difference. It's phenomenal. Something is up." Ryan gestured toward the chair for Erin to sit on the opposite side of the desk.

"We agree, something is up. Property values are plummeting. Have you found a common denominator yet?" Erin smoothed her skirt as she sat.

"Yes, I have. T & H Realty."

"Never heard of them," Erin said then leaned over and picked up a copy of a deed.

"I've scanned in copies of all the deeds, and I've made a spreadsheet with prices. It helps to compare them. Here, look." Ryan twisted the screen around where Erin could see it. The spreadsheet showed the appraised value and the actual sales price and the percentage of difference. “I took the appraised value from the assessor’s office. It might not be exactly what the land would sell for, but it is a good idea of value. As you can see, these properties sold for fifty percent of the value they should have sold for. Some less.”

Erin looked at the screen and then at the pile of printed deeds on the desk. “And they all sold to T & H Realty, LLC. I’ll look into who owns that. You’ve already done a ton of work here.” Erin leaned back from the computer screen. “Can you email a copy of that spreadsheet to me?”

Ryan glanced at the screen and then back up at Erin. “Yes, it’s almost finished. I’ll send it over pretty soon.”

Erin looked at Ryan. “You work in Tulsa but still live in Mannford?”

“Yes, I like being near the lake. I have an apartment there. It’s a short drive most mornings. And you?”

“No, I moved to Tulsa so I’m closer to work. But I run back and forth a lot, too. Mom still lives in Mannford.”

“How is your mom?”

“She’s good. Still managing the flower shop at the grocery store and dating the manager. They seem to have a good time. He’s a good guy.”

Erin stood. “I hate to run so quickly. And I’m glad someone else is working on this. It will save me a lot of time. It’s almost five o’clock, and I have to get back to the office. It was great to see you though. Maybe we can get a drink sometime and catch up?”

Ryan smiled. “Of course. That would be great. Remember the old floating restaurant called Pier 51? Do you have plans for later this week?”

“I haven’t been there in a while. Sounds good. Call me. My cell’s on the back of the card. We’ll get together.” She handed over her business card as she stood. Again, thanks for all the help.”

Erin walked out the door and rounded the corner as Ryan stared at the documents in front of her. Keystone Lake was being bought and sold at record speeds.

Thinking of the lake brought back memories of Chris. Maybe it was because she’d talked to Erin, someone else from her past. She hated the fact that everything made her think of Chris. She was desperate to see him again, and desperation never led her anywhere good. She knew she was stupid to get involved with Kenny after college, but she was devastated when Chris left. Desperate enough to do a lot of stupid things.

She had a few wild days in college after breaking up with Chris and ended up one night in a honkey-tonk bar with some of the girls from school—a place she shouldn’t have been. She should have been back in the apartment studying for finals. It didn’t take long for Kenny and his buddies to home in on the college girls out on the town. It was a whirlwind romance on the rebound after the breakup with Chris. Kenny quickly popped the question soon after graduation. She didn’t know him well enough. And the first time she came home from work to find him drunk in front of the television in the middle of the day, it began to dawn on her he was using her. He drifted from job to job, never working anywhere too long.

“What are you worried about, honey? You’re working. We have money.” Kenny slopped the beer on the recliner as he watched Nascar on the cable channel she paid for.

Thankfully, she was working, or how else would the bills have been paid? He'd moved in with her when they married and never had a plan to work very hard. It was okay with him, he said, if the little woman brought home the bacon.

Shaking her head to bring her back to reality, Ryan picked up the business card and emailed the spreadsheet to Erin. She felt Erin was a kindred spirit, and they had to find out what was going on with the lake properties.

Chapter 19

Erin stared at the pile of deeds in front of her that Ryan had emailed before she left the office last night. She printed them out and stuffed them in the file to be easy to look at, then searched the Secretary of State's website. She had the name of the LLC but needed to know who the Registered Agent and officers were. She was surprised to find the address was located in Mannford. Ted Shipley owed T & H Realty. And he was buying up flooded land from his neighbors.

Once she had a name, she dialed the number on the card Ryan had given her. It rang once, and the receptionist picked up then put her through quickly.

"Morning, Erin." Ryan sounded happy to hear from her.

"Hi, Ryan. How are you today?"

"Doing well. Glad you called. I needed a break from what I was doing." Ryan sighed. "What's up?"

Erin hoped this was good news. "I have some news. I've been on the Secretary of State's website and found out who owns T & H Realty. Maybe you know him? Ted Shipley."

There was a pause on the other end then Ryan cleared her throat. "Ted Shipley?"

"That's who they list as the Registered Agent," Erin said, twirling a pencil. "Do you know him?

"Everyone in Mannford does. Ted and Hope Shipley

are long-time residents of Mannford. Well, Hope is. Her maiden name was Beck. I really don't know how long Ted has lived here. I think he came here and met Hope and stayed. I can only assume he is the T in T & H, and that would mean the H stands for Hope."

Erin put down the pencil. Hope Beck was Chris' sister—Maggie's daughter. Were the Becks buying up Keystone Lake? No, the Secretary of State website said Shipley, not Beck. Hope was married, and her name was Shipley. "I know her, she's Chris Beck's sister. I remember her from school. In fact, I just saw them recently after their uncle's funeral."

"She married Shipley, and they live on the lake. He has been in real estate for a long time. I think she's a stay-at-home mom with several kids. You know the Becks? I guess you do, since you're from Mannford. Everybody does."

"I swam at their place when I was a kid. A lot of us did." Erin's head was spinning. Chris' sister was involved in a real estate scam—if there was one—and it appeared on paper as if there was. Did Chris know about this? "I knew Chris in high school. And I remember Hope. She was older than Chris. She wasn't around as much when I swam there. We were a younger bunch of kids than Hope. But I can't imagine her involved in what looks like a real estate scam. I mean the Becks are just good, salt-of-the earth people."

"Neither can I. I know the family and have always been fond of them."

Erin again picked up the pencil and twirled it in thought. "Do you think Chris' sister could be involved in a real estate scam? And what about Chris? Do you think he knows?"

"I don't know. People change. But not the Beck family I knew. I don't think they could have changed that much anyway."

Erin once more stared at the pile of deeds. "Maybe the Shipleys have motives we don't know about. I mean, the lake is in trouble, and maybe Shipley is just trying to help out his neighbors by buying their land so they can get out from under it."

There was silence on the other end. "Maybe. But since they don't have a lot of cash, and we know from the bank that Ted Shipley borrowed money to buy the land, it must have been a business deal that worked to his advantage. But I don't know him. Maybe I'm jumping to conclusions. Hope would never allow this if she thought her husband was cheating their neighbors."

"Then maybe she was unaware of what he was doing," Erin said.

Ryan slurped her coffee. "Maybe she was. I imagine five kids could keep her busy. But the bank has cut him off, according to my sources, so he is done buying land at this time."

Chapter 20

Chris wiped down the boat his parents loaned him once more. The windshield had been spattered with so much water spraying from the front of the boat he could barely see out. It was going to be tough leaving this lake where he grew up, but he had assignments waiting. He needed to get back. He should pull the boat out of the water and really clean it before he left if he could find time. Dad was gone so much, and Mom seldom took care of the boat, so it was really dirty. And so was he.

Pulling off the sweat-stained tee shirt, he tossed it on the back seat along with his shoes before putting down the ladder to climb into the dark water. The sun was setting on the other side of the lake and sparkled like diamonds on the calm water. A few fish flopped in the distance and, aside from that, he had the lake to himself. It was the middle of the week, and most people were home. The lake filled up on the weekends, but only the permanent residents were here during the week. He hadn't even seen any fishermen coming in with a catch. It was Tuesday—whatever that meant—and he enjoyed the calm as he stroked out to the middle of the cove and looked around.

He used to practically live in this cove as a kid. Mom and Dad had to pull him and Hope out of the water and shove them in the bathtub before dark during summer. Most nights after dinner on the deck they'd head back to the lake for one last swim before bed when the water was warm. He often “accidentally” fell in when it was too cold for swimming. It drove his mother crazy, but the lure of the water was just too much and called his name sometimes.

He lay floating on his back gently moving his arms to stay afloat and looked up at the few stars that were coming out in the evening sky and smiled. Could he find a way to make a living around here, he wondered? Would he be willing to leave the wide-open spaces for home?

“Watcha doin’?” A familiar voice from up on the dock called out to him in the water. Ryan? Here on his father’s dock? She walked to the end of the dock and sat down cross-legged in her jean shorts and stared out into the water. He instantly swam toward her—then slowed, trying not to appear too eager.

“Swimming,” he said as he got close enough to see the reflection of the last of the sunset on her red/gold tresses. “Want to join me? Did you bring your suit?”

“No.” She smiled once more as he got closer. The sun made one final burst through the trees and then sank for another night.

Chris could see Ryan’s silhouette as she once again stood up and looked down at him where he treaded water. Slowly, she pulled the tank top over her head. Tossing it into the boat tied to the dock. She unbuttoned the cut-off shorts (were those the ones she always wore when they were in high school?) and dropped them to the dock. Kicking them into the boat, she slowly reached behind and unfastened her bra. She giggled as she threw it in with the other clothes.

The scene reminded him of high school, and Chris

knew what was about to happen. At least he hoped he did.

Slowly she lowered her panties dropping them with the rest of the clothes. Lights from across the lake shown on the water and reflected off her supple body.

Chris wiped a hand across his lips as she stood before him like she had when they were younger, and she suddenly dove into the water like a mermaid. She came up behind him squirting him with water from her mouth.

"Well, hello," he said reaching for her and pulling her close. He was hooked—and he was sure she knew it. Chris dismissed the thought of mermaids pulling sailors down to their deaths as he kissed her lips. Memories flooded back to nights on the lake after climbing out of his bedroom window. As teenagers they were drawn to each other like moths to a flame. And then in college when she wanted to get married, he balked. The world called to him, and he longed to see it. Photography was his love. His first love? Or was Ryan his first love? That became the sticking point between them. His wanderlust left her behind, and he knew he was the reason for the breakup.

Kissing her neck, he gently pushed her against the boat, and she reached a hand behind him pulling off his trunks, tossing them into the stern of the boat. She then latched onto the vessel gently rocking in the waves they made. The only sound in the cove was their deep breathing and an occasional slosh of the boat against the dock.

Whispering sweet nothings, they made promises they might not be able to keep. The fire was still there—as well as the love. The years seemed like minutes since he'd held her in his arms—nothing had changed in the way he felt, and he wondered if she felt the same. Or maybe this was her way of getting back at him for leaving her. He hoped not. He'd regretted many times leaving her behind, but he had another love that needed him too.

She trembled. "I still love you," she whispered finally and readjusted her hold on the rocking boat—one hand on the stern and one on the pier of the dock. The moon shone on her face as he pulled back and looked at her.

"I love you, too. What was I thinking leaving you like that?" He kissed her deeply, and she sighed then turned to climb the ladder into the boat. He followed and watched as she dressed, his trunks hung limp in his hand as he drip dried in the night air. Suddenly realizing he was naked, he pulled on the wet trunks and dirty tee shirt then reached for her as he sat on the seat of the boat and pulled her into his lap.

"I can't believe you did that." Chris kissed Ryan's neck, laying his head against her shoulder, smelling her freshly washed skin underneath the slight scent of lake water. She was still moist where he touched her, and her shirt stuck to her back. There were no towels for drying in the boat, so they had dressed still dripping.

"What? You didn't like it?" Ryan shook back wet hair and pulled it into a bun at the back of her neck, then let it go again.

"You know I did. It's been a long time." Chris could not believe this woman sat in his lap again. The woman he sent packing years ago because he was too scared of being tied down. He must have been crazy.

Chris stared into her eyes in the available light. "Hungry?" He brushed drying hair from her face as they sat in the moonlight on the gently rocking boat.

"Nothing has changed. You're always hungry after sex. Or maybe you're just always hungry. Anyway, I'm wet and can't go into a restaurant like this."

"I was thinking of Mom's kitchen. There's always food there. If nothing else, we could fix a piece of toast. You have no idea how wonderful the convenience of a toaster can be. Even sliced bread."

"It was your idea to discover the world. And there are lots of places in the world without the convenience of a toaster."

"Yeah, I was an idiot. Probably still am. But I'm a hungry idiot, so join me?" Chris stood and placed Ryan back on her feet. The warmth of her body still on his legs, he led her out of the boat and up on the dock.

Inside his mother's kitchen the house was dark. Mom and Dad had gone to bed. He could see the light of the television coming from their bedroom door. Sometimes they fell asleep with it on, especially when Dad was home.

They sat at the kitchen table and talked quietly while sharing the nibbles he found in his mother's refrigerator—just like they had when they were teenagers.

Chapter 21

Ralph Larson was an engineer by trade. He understood how things worked. He made a good living for himself and his family over the years. With his daughter graduated from college and his wife often convalescing from the effects of Lupus, he found he had a lot of time on his hands these days. He also found he loved to sail. The small boat he bought a few years ago was just for him. He had to admit it. His daughter, Bernadette, was at TU at the time, and his wife, Francesca, no longer worked. He would sometimes get her out on the water in good weather for short periods when her body would allow it. But the boat was really for him.

Engineering was a good trade, but he didn't have the drive for money and success he once had. He had faced death—that of his daughter's and the eventuality of his wife's. And that changed everything. The potential death of the two people in the world he loved the most was worse than the thought of his own. Francesca couldn't live forever with a debilitating disease. And then there was Bernadette. While still in college she was kidnapped by a nutcase and tied up in the tunnels that ran under downtown Tulsa. But she was a fighter like her mother. Somehow, she managed to get free and come home to testify against the man who kidnapped her. Now she was about to become a mother—making him a grandfather.

How could that happen? How could his little girl be having a child? Well, he knew how. The child's father, a long-time boyfriend who had been in and out of Ralph's house for years, panicked and ran for the hills as soon as he saw the plus sign on the pregnancy test. Who would have thought?

Ralph was a young man once, and he remembered how hormones could run the show, but he couldn't imagine leaving someone you loved just because you got scared. Bernadette, on the other hand, said she would provide for the little one and herself without the father. The boyfriend had no part in her life anymore. But Ralph did. He'd set aside a trust fund for Bernadette years ago when she was born and probably needed to talk to his financial advisor about doing the same for the new addition to their family.

The light breeze blew against his face as his boat glided over sparkling water. The sun was warm but not yet hot. It was a wet spring, and the water levels in the lake were rising again. Just when they were about to get back to normal, they rose once more. He needed to talk to his friend at the Corps of Engineers and find out what was wrong with the dam. Was it clogged up, or were there political reasons why the lake seemed to be in trouble this year? Politics always played a part, even in his small town. Soon the tourists would quit coming if they couldn't play on their favorite playground. There were other lakes in the state, and they would just go to them. The problem needed to be fixed—and soon.

His cousin Jeff recently died on this lake. He was a good swimmer and boater—an excellent fisherman. It was unlikely that he just fell overboard and drowned, but that was how the sheriff saw it. However, Ralph knew

Jeff was a drunk, and maybe that was the problem. Ralph wondered if the condition of the lake had anything to do with Jeff's death. They would probably never know.

The stump of a tree floated upside down in the water ahead casting a shadow on the ripples. It was amazing the things that once lay on dry land that were now floating in the lake. Ralph cautiously swerved around it. He was too close to the shore—or where the shore used to be. He slowly came about and maneuvered the boat with the wind to his back. Francesca would have lunch ready soon, and he should be getting the boat back to the marina.

The bump wasn't loud, but it rocked the boat from side to side. Invisible debris in the water was dangerous. A loud screeching sound down the side of the boat reminded Ralph of fingernails on a blackboard. Carefully moving more closely to the center of the cove, he exited and headed for the marina. The large limb he ran over popped up from the back of the boat and rolled in the dark brown muddy water. He would have the boat checked out when he got back. He didn't need a hole in the fiberglass hull.

He lowered the sail and started the small engine to help him edge the boat into the tight space. The marina, with all the other boats, was no place to depend upon the wind. He pulled deftly into the slot marked Larson 512 then cut the engine. His slip was easy to find because it was next to a small replica of a seventeenth century pirate's ship painted black and white with gold trim. The British Royal Navy would have been proud of it, at least until it was taken over by hoodlums who might make them walk the plank.

The rubber bumpers helped to protect the body of

the boat as it nudged the sides of the slip. Water slopped from side to side and rocked his favorite plaything. Ralph jumped off and tied the boat in place then walked around to the side of his boat to see if he could find any damage. It looked like just a scratch in the paint and not a big one at that. He would talk to Smitty about checking it out sometime soon. If he could find him. Smitty hadn't been at his shop much lately. Ralph hated to wait on the bigger shops who only wanted to sell him something newer. He just needed repairs, not another boat. He found Smitty in his phone contacts and pushed dial.

The phone rang all the way up the ramp and into the parking lot, but Smitty never answered. Again. Ralph would have to find someone else to check out his boat, he thought pocketing the cell phone. He hoped Smitty was okay.

A young woman with dark hair stood by his truck when he got to the parking lot.

"I thought I might find you here." Erin smiled.

Erin Sampson was a girl he'd known most of her life. She was his daughter's best friend. "Erin! It's so good to see you." He hugged her closely and then stepped back. "To what do I owe this visit?"

"I wanted to talk with you if I could—as an engineer. I have a question."

"Shoot." He unlocked the door and climbed in starting the engine, then cranked up the air conditioner. Leaning back over the top of the truck he spoke to Erin. "You want to sit?" He gestured toward the other side of the truck.

Erin climbed into the small pickup.

"So, what's so important that you hunt me down at my boat. You certainly know where I live."

"I'm working on a case and needed some expert advice. I called your house, and Francesca said I could find you here."

"You're on a case, huh? Who do you represent?"

"Sunset Hills Homeowners' Association has hired our firm to look into the lake levels and the sale of property around the lake. I needed an engineer to explain a few things to me. Is the dam discharging enough water? I mean I know it's been raining a lot and there is runoff from the rivers upstream making matters worse, but the lake levels are so high, and it seems like the dam is not running as well as it should. It's not letting out a lot of water."

"I was just thinking about talking to the Corps of Engineers myself. I have a friend there, name of Rogers. Young fella. Not from around here—back east somewhere. I could ask him and, if we don't get some satisfaction, we could bring it up at the next Town Hall meeting. I think it's next Tuesday. Maybe you should be there. But you're right. There is too much water in this lake, and the last time I was by the dam it didn't seem much water was being released. I just ran over a stump hidden underwater and scraped up the boat. I'm not alone. Boaters are getting tired of not being able to use their lake anymore or, if they do, the constant repairs from damage. People spend a lot of money on boats, and they want to protect them."

"Yeah, I don't blame them. Tuesday night, huh? I may have to visit the town meeting. You want to join me?"

"Of course. But first, how about coming home and having lunch with us?"

"That would be great, and then I'd get to see

Francesca."

Chapter 22

"Okay, I'm bringing the City of Mannford townhall meeting to order." The gavel banged on the makeshift desk in the police department as the mayor tried to get the attention of those in the room. It was a small gathering. The usual ones.

Ted Shipley sat at the back of the meeting listening intently. He thought most towns had such a group of people who kept on top of things. Maybe they were worried about how the town was run, or maybe they just liked the power of being in charge. For whatever reason they attended, they were there, and he needed to stay on top of how they felt about things if his dream were to come to reality.

"Madam Secretary, will you read the minutes of the last meeting?" The mayor began once more.

Shipley watched the bright red bushy hair float around the secretary's face as she began to read, when the back door to the meeting opened. A young woman in jeans stepped in the room followed by Ralph and Chris.

"Are there any corrections to the minutes?" There was a short, silent pause. "If there are no corrections, the minutes are approved as read." The mayor sat and shuffled through his paperwork.

Shipley wondered if anyone really listened, but still, they didn't disapprove the minutes.

The mayor stood once more and cleared his throat.

"I think we should cut to the chase. Most of you are here today to talk about the dam and the lake levels." He nodded to the few who had just come in the door. Most of the rest of the people in the room twisted around to look with curiosity at the newcomers.

"I see we have some guests who normally don't attend these meetings. I'm sure most of you know Ralph Larson and Chris Beck. Chris is a local celebrity."

A few chuckles rose from the crowd.

Any head that had not turned around before now was staring at the late comers to the meeting as they nodded. "But I'm not sure who the other one is." The mayor squinted at the back of the room.

Erin stood. "Mayor, I'm Erin Sampson with Cronkite and Associates. Our law firm represents Sunset Hills Homeowners' Association. The members of the association are concerned about the condition of their lake and want to be sure it is taken care of."

"Well, I assure you, Ms. Sampson, that the city of Mannford is taking excellent care of Keystone Lake."

The people of the room grumbled at the interruptions as they shifted in their seats.

"Mr. Mayor," Erin began again, "the association is concerned about the water levels of their lake and property being sold at record low rates."

"Now, wait just a minute," the mayor began. "Keystone Lake is a Corps of Engineers Lake and doesn't belong to the homeowners' association. Let's get that straight right up front. And we, as custodians of the lake in our town, are very proud of the job we do in looking after the lake."

Shipley smiled as the mayor began to waffle, his position being challenged. And the crowd grumbled more loudly.

"I'm sure you are, Mayor. But the people who own land around the lake are concerned for their property and those of their neighbors. They'd like to know why the lake levels are so high and why the dam isn't doing its job letting out the water more quickly." Erin paused to let the mayor answer her question.

"Now, ma'am, we're sure the dam is working at full capacity and as I'm sure you know it has been raining a lot this year. We not only get the rainfall but the runoff from both the Cimarron and Arkansas Rivers. I don't know if you're from around here…"

"I grew up in Mannford, Mr. Mayor. I graduated from Mannford High, Erin Sampson. I now live and work in Tulsa, but I am a former resident. My mother still lives and works here. I may not be a resident anymore, but I represent the residents of this lake."

The mayor once more squinted at the back of the room then put on his glasses.

"I am feeling old. Erin Sampson, I remember you. Kids grow up, don't they? And sometimes they leave home. You don't live here anymore, but still, you're back and in the middle of a hometown meeting."

"Mr. Mayor, Ralph Larson here." Ralph stood in the back of the room.

"We all know who you are, Ralph," The mayor said slowly letting the air out of his lungs.

Ralph began again. "I'm still a resident, and I'm here with some questions of my own. As many of you know, I'm an engineer, and I too, am concerned about the dam. It's old. Built around 1960, even older than me. And as an engineer I'd like to ask if a structural assessment of the dam has been done lately. And if not, why? We have some concerns as to the safety of the lake, the dam, and the homes around it."

The room erupted into members all asking questions at the same time. The mayor tried to answer them as they were thrown at him. Giving up he once more banged the gavel. This time with more authority.

"Okay, that's enough. Quiet down or I'll clear the room." He banged the gavel so hard Shipley was afraid the handle would fly off.

Participants turned around and slowly began to quiet.

"Ralph, did you have something in mind? Like I said, this is a Corps of Engineers lake and doesn't belong to the City of Mannford."

"I talked to a friend at the Corps and asked him if he thought the dam was in trouble. He said it had been discussed and they were planning a check of the dam. They're going to send some divers down to look into the inner workings. After all there's only so much you can do from up top. Maybe the bottom of the dam needs inspection too."

"Mr. Mayor," Chris stood from his seat at the back. "As you said earlier, I'm Chris Beck, and I don't live here anymore but my parents, sister, and brother-in-law do." Chris nodded to Shipley. "I'm back for my uncle's funeral. I'm a certified scuba diver, and we talked to the Corps of Engineers about checking the dam. Of course, they have a diver too, but I'd like to accompany him. We've set it up for early Saturday morning, and we wanted to let everyone know why the dam would be shut down at that time for a few hours."

"You boys got it all under control, don't you?" The mayor shifted in his seat looking uncomfortable. "I mean why did you come here if the Corps is taking care of it?"

"My parents are landowners around the lake too, which is why I went to the Corps with Ralph. I wanted you to know we're not trying to go around you. We know you're concerned about the lake too. But we just decided to try to find out what's going on, and we wanted you to know our intentions. We plan to report back our findings."

"See that you do. We in Mannford are concerned for the lake too. And if the Corps wants to do an inspection, and they don't mind Chris tagging along, then that is their business. But be sure you let us know what you find out."

Shipley shifted in his seat; the smile replaced with a look of concern. He didn't need the Corps of Engineers finding the extra zebra mussels Decker dumped into the specific spot on the dam and undertaking a cleaning project. His timing on the dam destruction was right on schedule.

Chapter 22

Tossing the anchor over the side, Chris and Engineer Rogers surveyed the behemoth concrete structure before them. Chris had never been this close to the dam before. At least not from the water. Boaters were kept at a greater distance for safety's sake by way of a floating buoy and cable. But the time had come for some manual checking to see why the dam was not operating as it should.

"I appreciate you helping out with this," Rogers said as he pulled on his buoyancy compensator vest with his air tank in the back.

Chris' old wet suit had hung in the closet at his parents' house for years and, miracle of miracles, it still fit. All that hiking to remote places had paid off. He was still thin even into his late 20s. The remaining equipment he borrowed from the Corps.

"It's been a while, but I think I can still remember how this is done." Chris smiled at the man he had met only yesterday when he and Dad traveled to the office of the Corps of Engineers. Ralph and Paul insisted that the dam was clogged, or it would have been letting out water more efficiently. And it needed to be inspected from under the surface, not just from the instruments up top. And Chris offered to help since the Corps only had one diver available on site.

After checking equipment, Chris and Rogers waddled to the back of the boat with their fins on. Then with regulators in their mouths and one hand securing their masks, they did a giant stride into the water while Paul and the other ranger watched from the front of the boat. Adjusting their regulators and masks, Rogers nodded to the dam and, dumping the air out of his BC, descended into the dark murky water.

Chris followed, flipping on the photo-video light attached to his hand. It had a broad beam and covered a large area, but it was like bright lights on a foggy night. Keystone lake was not a clear diver's paradise. It had a sandy and muddy bottom, not rock like some lakes.

The cool, quiet water reminded Chris he needed to get back into scuba diving. It had been a while, but the quiet serenity of the water always calmed him. If this had been the clear blue Caribbean, he might never have resurfaced. As it was, he had a job to do, and he followed the dim yellow of the flippers and air tank belonging to the man from the Corps of Engineers, determined not to lose him. The murky water could be disorienting.

And there it was. The giant wall of concrete before him was the Keystone Dam, open for business in 1968. How many tons of concrete had been poured here? Several small communities had been abandoned to make way for the flooding that happened after the dam was erected. It had been a boon to the economy but maybe not the towns it covered with water.

The huge round intake control gates held his gaze in awe. He'd researched that in advance and found they were 27 feet in diameter. That made them wide enough across to suck in at least four divers laid end to end, but the Corps had been certain all suction had been turned off. The size and power of the dam finally impacted Chris like a cannon ball to the stomach. If it hadn't been for the mouthpiece where he drew oxygen, his mouth would have dropped open. Knowing the size was one thing, but seeing it face to face, another.

He could still see the yellow fins and tanks belonging to Rogers as he shone his flashlight toward the control tanks, and Chris swam up beside him. The metal guard on the outside of the intake was covered with crustaceans—zebra mussels. Knocking a few off with his gloved hand, he shone his flashlight into the intake. It looked like a nursery of tiny shells clumped one on top of the other. When the intakes were switched on, the shells were sucked into the workings of the dam.

If it was this bad on the outside, how bad was the inside of the dam and where the water rushed out?

Rogers moved on down the row of control gates on the dam and shone his flashlight into each of them. The intakes all looked clogged with crustaceans that reproduced at a rapid rate. The dam gave the adults everything they needed to secure the newborns in their nursery.

At the end of the row, Rogers held up a hand and then pointed back the way they came. Chris followed the glowing flippers back to the area of the boat. They had their answer. Zebra mussels were growing with abandon. And the dam was in trouble if they couldn't be eradicated.

Chapter 23

Erin threw her briefcase and keys on the coffee table and inhaled the aroma of food. Good food. Not the drive-through stuff they usually came home with. Rob was cooking!

"Hi, babe!" Rob called from the kitchen. He appeared in the doorway wearing the frilly apron that Erin's grandmother had made, with a huge red stain down the front and a spoon in hand. "Try this." Rob raised one eyebrow and smiled.

Rob tried to cook now and then since she worked long hours, but she encouraged him to stick to the simple stuff. Who knew what he'd prepared tonight?

Lightly touching her tongue to the end of the spoon, she tested it for heat. Rob loved the hot sauce. "Yum!" She grabbed his end of the spoon and shoved it in her mouth. "That's great. You made that?"

Rob frowned. "Well, I heated up the jar of spaghetti sauce. But I'm pretty sure you're supposed to taste it if you're a great chef." Handing her the spoon, he pulled the garlic bread from the oven placing it on the countertop. "You like it huh? Not too hot for you?"

"It's perfect. Let me change, and I'll be right back." Erin raced to the bedroom pulling off her jacket as she went. In the bedroom she tiptoed around the boxes of wedding invitations and samples of fabric for bridesmaid dresses as she kicked off her shoes and pulled clothes from the drawer.

She quickly reappeared in the kitchen wearing shorts and a tee shirt. Rob had placed the food on the kitchen table and was burning his finger trying to light the one lonely candle that stood sentry in the middle of the food.

"How was your day?" she asked, folding the napkin in her lap.

Without tasting the food, Rob doused it with hot sauce. "Good. And yours?"

"Good." She sprinkled parmesan cheese on top of the pile of spaghetti she knew was too much too eat. She twirled the noodles on a fork and raised them to her mouth before speaking. "Do you remember the Becks from high school? Chris and Hope?"

"Yeah." Rob talked with a mouth full of spaghetti. It dripped down his shirt. The dirty apron now draped over the sink.

She swallowed her bite. "Did you like them?"

Rob wiped his chin of sauce. "I think. I remember Chris was cool. They were both older than us." He paused. "Hope was oldest, wasn't she? I mean I can't remember much about her. What do you remember?"

"I used to hang out with them when I was young because they had a boat dock. We swam there some, and I had a crush on Chris. He was older than me, and I was just a kid." Erin smiled shyly at Rob. "I found out something lately that astounds me. I wanted to see what you thought." She sipped the instant iced tea with two ice cubes floating on top that Rob had made for her.

Rob shoved garlic bread in his mouth. "A crush huh? Okay, I'll bite." He smiled. "What did you find out?"

"This is between us, of course."

Rob nodded.

Erin swirled spaghetti on the end of her fork choosing her words before she spoke. "This has nothing to do with the crush. And that was a long time ago, anyway. You're safe. You know a lot of people have left the lake since the water levels have been up, and property is for sale? It appears there may be a real estate scam in the works. You know all the prime land is underwater these days with the lake so high. Some say artificially high." She took another drink. "It might be that the Becks or Shipleys are behind it."

Rob dropped his fork, and spaghetti sauce splattered across the table.

"I said, might be. You know. It hasn't been proven yet."

Wiping up the mess, Rob looked up. "The Chris Beck I knew would never do something like that."

"No, not Chris. Hope and her husband, Ted Shipley. Her maiden name was Beck, but now it's Shipley." Erin placed the wound-up spaghetti noodles in her mouth and chewed.

"Wow. I didn't know her, but I knew Chris, and the family seemed like nice people. I don't remember what her dad did, but he was gone a lot. Her mother taught at a college somewhere, I think. I don't know what she taught. But they lived on the lake and commuted into Tulsa or something." Rob stared off into space. "I can't believe this. How did you find out?"

"Like I said, it's not proven, and you can't say anything, but I thought you might know them. I'm representing the homeowners of Sunset Hills, and they asked me to look into property sales. The accounting firm Ryan Wendler works for is putting all this together, and I talked to her this week. Do you remember her? We haven't seen each other in a long time. Ryan also mentioned that maybe he was trying to help his neighbors by purchasing their land that was currently underwater. I doubt it, but stranger things have happened. Anyway, Ryan and I agreed to meet for a drink. I keep expecting her to call. Do you want to go if she does?"

"Ryan Windler, now there's a name I haven't heard in a while. She and Chris used to be really thick. Everyone always thought they'd marry, and then he ran off to who knows where. I don't know what happened to them. But she's working on this case too? How does she feel about the Becks?"

Erin shrugged. "She didn't mention that she and Chris used to date. I find that interesting. Anyway, I guess the bank got leery and asked the accounting firm to look into it. Too much land going from hand to hand too quickly or something." Erin's phone buzzed. "And there she is. It's Ryan, want to go with me? This could be good."

"Too much work," he said nodding to the paperwork on the couch and taking his plate to the sink. "Maybe next time."

****

The light breeze blew Erin's hair away from her face as she stared out onto the lake she'd loved as long as she could remember. The sun set slowly, and she waited for Ryan to arrive. She swirled the beer—the amber light reflecting off the glass—when she heard someone a few tables behind her began talking on a phone.

"The biologist at the university said zebra mussels

will clog up and ruin a lake," the man on the phone said. "They travel from boat to boat and can ruin an outboard motor as well as something as big as a dam. You did the right thing. If someone comes snooping around wondering about the operation of the dam, we can blame the zebra mussels."

It wasn't a voice Erin recognized, and she hated to turn around. Mannford was a small town and having grown up there she knew most of the people, but she'd lived in Tulsa for a while, and there were some new faces in her childhood home. But this voice didn't sound familiar.

Ryan walked across the deck of the floating restaurant searching the diners and quickly waved. Stopping several times to greet people as she crossed to where Erin was, she finally sat just as the waitress arrived.

"Whatever's on tap," she said. The waitress nodded back to her. "Are you hungry?"

Erin brushed her hair from her eyes. "Sorry, Rob had dinner ready when I got in, and I had to eat it. He is so proud when he cooks, and tonight it was good. I've finally convinced him to leave the jar of spaghetti sauce alone. It's fine as it is. Not everything needs hot sauce."

"So, you and Rob are still an item? It must be nice to be in love with someone so long and still be together."

"Well, we didn't really start dating until college. We were just friends before that."

The waitress set the beer in front of Ryan, who then took a long sip. "Even better, couples should be friends."

"Rob is great. He waited for me a long time, and we've set a wedding date for Christmas when his family can all be here. I wanted a small wedding in my mom's back yard, but Rob's family wanted the church and all the family. The event is growing. My mom is doing the flowers of course and my friend, Bernadette, is in charge of the dresses, so they might be unusual!" Erin laughed. "But seriously, she is a fantastic designer. I just have to keep a close eye on what she decides everyone should wear. I haven't seen the final sketch yet, but I know it will be memorable."

"Wow, a family wedding with designer dresses, it sounds wonderful."

From the table behind her a male voice said, "You just make sure that no one finds out—and do your job!" A chair screeched across the floor, and a man pushed past them toward the door tossing bills at the waitress as he left.

Erin cleared her throat. "Wow. He's in a hurry."

Ryan took a drink and swallowed. "That's Ted Shipley." She gave Erin a knowing look. "Chris' brother-in-law. I don't know him very well. But I know him when I see him." She nodded after him, cleared her throat, and spoke again. "I'm starving. How about some nachos?"

Erin set her glass on the table. "I just ate, but you go ahead."

Ryan paused. "If you're sure you don't mind, I guess." She waved the waitress back over. "I'll order the chicken nachos." The waitress nodded and walked away writing on her notebook.

Erin sipped her beer. "I overheard him on the phone before you got here saying something about zebra mussels and how they can clog up a dam and boat motors. That's not news to anyone on this lake. But the way he said it to the person on the other end was like they had something to hide about the dam and trying to use the zebra mussels to cover it up. I need to see what I can find out about Shipley and maybe see if there is a problem with the dam."

Ryan nodded. "It seems weird that we are checking up on our neighbors. But I think you may be right."

The evening became quiet, and Erin looked around at the darkening lake then cleared her throat. "Ryan, I heard by the grapevine that you and Chris used to be close." Erin looked closely at the woman over the top of her glass.

"We dated in school. Actually, I thought we were going to get married, but he bailed." Ryan sipped her drink. "I went to see him this week since I knew he was in town. I think he was happy to see me."

Erin swallowed her beer. "Great. I hope it goes well for you. If that's what you want."

"I really don't know what I want." Ryan swigged a large amount of beer. "But back to Ted Shipley, we know T & H Realty, LLC's name was on all those deeds around the lake. And we know that T & H Realty, LLC is owned by Ted and Hope Shipley. We also know that the parcels of land were purchased at rock bottom prices because of all the flooding. We can prove all of that. But what does Ted Shipley have to do with the dam if anything?"

Erin frowned and placed her glass on the table. "I don't know. But I wonder if the Corps of Engineers does. You think someone there will talk to us?"

Chapter 24

"US Army Corps of Engineers, Keystone Lake," said the bored voice on the other end of the phone. The words all ran together as one, and Erin had to listen carefully to make them out.

"Is this Keystone Dam?" Erin asked hoping she didn't sound stupid. But what did he say?

"Yes ma'am. You've got the dam. What can I do for you?"

"This is Erin Sampson of Cronkite and Associates out of Tulsa. I was wanting to talk to the Chief Engineer. Is that you?"

"No ma'am, the chief is at lunch and due back about 1:30. Can I take a message?"

He still sounded bored. Most people perked up when they found out she was a lawyer. Maybe they thought they were in trouble. But at least she knew when the chief would be back.

"No, no message. I'll drop by after he gets back. I need to talk to him about the dam."

"Okay, that'll be after 1:30. Anything else?"

"No, that's it. Thank you." She hung up.

One thirty. That gave her time to get some lunch and get to the dam. Perfect. She needed to talk to the operators at the dam to see if there was a problem. The clients were concerned, and she was beginning to agree with them. Not only was the dam not operating as it should, but properties were also changing hands too quickly.

She told the receptionist where she was going, grabbed her purse, and headed for the door.

It was a quick trip from downtown Tulsa to the dam, and she could get a bite to eat along the way at her favorite floating restaurant. The water soothed her, and the day was beautiful.

"Cheeseburger and iced tea," she said as the waitress came up to the table with a menu in hand. She knew what she wanted. She sat in the sun watching the ducks in the water on their endless, yet lazy, search for food. Fishermen came and went with their boats, and some fueled at the end of the shop near the restaurant. Pier 51 did a booming business sometimes, especially on holiday weekends, but today she was the only diner. It was lunch time, and most businesspeople didn't come to the lake to eat.

It didn't take long for her lunch to arrive, and she sat staring out into the water as she ate. What was wrong with the lake she grew up on? Why was it flooding, other than the spring rains? The dam used to be able to handle runoff from the rains. And where were the people who used to live here?

Glancing at her watch, she tossed the rest of the burger on the plate and walked to the register to pay. If she hurried, she could catch the chief as he came in before he had a chance to leave again. Climbing in her car, she left the restaurant.

"I'm Erin Sampson here to see the Chief Engineer. I called earlier." The man behind the desk nodded to the young man in the office next door. "That's him."

Erin walked in knocking on his door. The name of

the Chief Engineer was Rogers, or that was what it said on his name tag. He didn't bother to introduce himself. He seemed in a hurry.

"You're the attorney. Yeah, I heard you were coming. I don't have much time. I need to get to the dam for the afternoon rounds but can spare a few minutes. What is this about?"

The man had an accent from back east somewhere. Not Oklahoma, and sometimes locals didn't take well to outsiders. She wondered if that fact gave him trouble in her home state. "I represent the homeowners at Sunset Hills, and they've asked me to check into the lake. It has been flooding a lot this year."

"We've had a lot of rain." The engineer fidgeted as he stood from his desk and looked ready to run if things got heated.

"I agree. I grew up in Mannford. I live in Tulsa now, and I know this lake. But we've had rain before. This year seems different. Do you think the dam is okay, or is it in structural trouble? It's not letting out the water as fast as it might. I mean is it working correctly?"

"My dam is fine, ma'am. Yes, it's old and hasn't had an upgrade for a few years, but it was built in 1968. It's over 50 years old. I think it works just fine for its age. And you know this is a Corps of Engineer lake, not a recreational lake. We provide hydroelectric power, and we sell that power and the water to our customers. I'm sorry if your jet ski is not liking all this water, but like I said, recreation is not the main reason the lake is here. I have to go do the afternoon run on the gauges. So, if you'll excuse me." He walked toward the door where she still stood and glanced out his window at the view of the monstrous dam—probably to avoid her gaze.

"Could I join you? I've never seen the inside of the dam."

"We have tours now and then. You might check into that if you're interested. There's a schedule at the front desk. But tell the homeowners, they have nothing to worry about. The US Army Corps of Engineers is on the job."

Erin stepped back as he breezed past and out the front door. She knew Aunt Toni would have never stood for that attitude. But at the moment, she didn't have anything to detain him with.

She watched him walk away and knew she had to make a move. Thank goodness she'd changed to her flats. Out the door, she strode up beside him as he headed for the stairs at the bottom of the dam.

"So, Chief Rogers, how long have you been an engineer? It seems you and I got off on the wrong foot. I'm not looking for trouble. I just want to be sure that the dam is safe. And I think you're the guy to talk to about such things." Sometimes you had to schmooze them a little.

He stopped, turned, and looked her up and down. He might have been a few years older than her, in his 30s, but he didn't have a military attitude. He was probably a civilian contractor. "You're really going to follow me, aren't you?" He began to sprint up the stairs.

Erin chased after him as quickly as she could. The gym membership had been a good idea. Sitting at a desk could kill you. "Yes, I need to see how this works. Like I said, I'm not looking for trouble. My clients aren't planning a lawsuit. But as a former resident of Mannford, where the lake sits, and a current resident of Tulsa, where the water flows down to, I think I have a right to know.

Is our dam in trouble and, if so, what's being done about it?" Erin's Aunt Toni had always said her tenacity was a good thing. She hoped so this time because she was beginning to breath heavily. But so was the engineer, she noticed.

The engineer halted his step. "You know there was a resident here lately who asked the same questions. I'm sorry to say he died in an accident—Jeff somebody. I was to meet him at the dam the night he drowned. I left him a voice mail about meeting at the dam, and he never showed. I guess now I know why. But I was planning to show him how safe our dam is. Now, I guess you can take his place. You can have a tour if it will get you to go away. Like I said, I have work to do so it has to be quick."

"Jeff Larson. I knew him. He was a long-time resident of Mannford—he and his family. His death was a great shame. I didn't know he had been planning on a tour of the dam. His family said he was concerned about the health of the lake and fishing."

Rogers stopped and looked at Erin. "I'm sorry. I didn't know you knew him. That was insensitive of me. I am sorry he died."

"There would be no way for you to know that we were acquainted. But Mannford is a small town, and everyone who lives here knows everyone else. I used to play at Jeff and his sister's house when I was a kid. His death was a great shock, and many people don't think it was an accident. Jeff was too savvy about water safety."

"I don't know anything about his death. Again, I'm sorry." The engineer continued up the concrete steps. He paused. "This is where I normally go into my spiel about the dam." He cleared his throat. "The Keystone Lake project was authorized by the Flood Control Act of 1950. It was designed and built by the Tulsa District, Army Corps of Engineers. Construction began in January 1957 and was completed in September 1964. Commercial operation of the power generating facility began in May 1968. The total project cost approximately $123 million." He smiled when he finished his speech and finished his climb up the last few steps.

At the top of the stairs, he pulled a ring of keys from his pocket inserting one into the metal door. He twisted the key and then opened the door. Stepping in he nodded for her to follow and flipped on the light switches beside the door. Slowly fluorescent lights came on down a long concrete hallway lined with gauges and switches.

Erin shadowed the engineer. He grabbed a clip board off the hook just inside the door and, with the pencil that dangled by a string, he began to walk down the hallway marking off a slot for each gauge on the paper.

Erin followed not knowing what she was looking at. Huge dials and levers were the controls for millions of gallons of water as it was held back until just the proper time for release. She was sure it also measured the amount of electricity created by the rushing water—electricity that powered the city down below and others.

The tour took less time than she thought. The engineer offered no more explanation other than his history lesson for what he was doing or the function of each piece of equipment. She followed him down the hallway and back up the other side. The inside of the dam smelled of mold and moisture though the concrete looked dry. When they once more reached the open door where they had entered, Rogers stopped and looked at her.

"Did that satisfy you? It is a long tunnel with gauges. Just what you thought, huh?"

"Pretty much. Thank you for the tour."

He gestured for her to step out first. As she walked around him, she bumped her hip on a cabinet that stuck out from the wall knocking the door ajar. "Sorry," she said shoving a cardboard tube back inside and closing the door. She walked out into the blinding sunlight.

****

After meeting the new Chief at the Corps of Engineers, Erin had even more questions. Maybe she needed to talk to the sheriff. Even though Jeff's death probably had nothing to do with her homeowners' association case, something made her think maybe it was connected. There were so many things going on in her hometown, and she needed to find out if they were connected in any manner.

Before heading back to the office, she stopped at the sheriff's office. She'd known Sheriff Montgomery since she was a child, and hopefully he'd remember her.

She stepped into the cool yet cluttered office of the sheriff. There was no receptionist sitting behind the wooden desk. Wood-paneled walls held pictures of the American flag and maps of the lake and county. Not much in the way of interior design.

"Hello?" she called out as she walked toward the office that opened on the other side of the room.

"Come on in," called the gruff voice she knew from years ago. A balding head appeared at the door, and a large smile covered the face of the man who once bowled on Saturday nights with her dad.

"Sheriff Montgomery." She smiled. She'd never

called him anything but that.

"Erin Sampson! Now it's been a while, girl. What are you doing in Mannford? I thought you lived in Tulsa." He stepped to her and enveloped her in a huge bear hug. He was a large man, and that was probably the only way he knew to do it.

But Erin didn't mind. He was always protective and like a second father to her. He'd been at their door immediately when her father died and more than once helped her mom with chores around the house when they were getting on their feet. "I do live and work in Tulsa now, but I come home now and then."

"What can I do for you?" He gestured to the lone wooden chair that sat on the opposite side of his desk.

Erin sat. "I represent Sunset Hills Homeowners' Association. And I've been doing a lot of digging around. I've found out that T & H Realty is buying up a lot of the land that has changed hands around here lately."

The sheriff raised one eyebrow. "Ok. I don't think I've heard of T & H Realty. Are they from around here?"

"Yes. T & H Realty, LLC is owned by Ted and Hope Shipley. Hope's maiden name was Beck."

Montgomery stopped the coffee cup halfway to his lips, setting it back down on the stained ring where it had last sat. "I know Ted and Hope, but they own a realty company? I mean I didn't know they had that kind of money. Real estate sales must be good."

"I don't know about money, but their names are on the LLC paperwork. I understand the bank has cut him off lately. But the LLC has managed to buy up property at rock bottom prices. Hope's uncle just died in an unusual manner—well unusual for Jeff. Maybe he just drowned and maybe not. I don't know if you've closed that case. But the Becks have been on this lake a long time. They're good people. Not the real estate scam type. And I was just wondering if there is a connection between the lake flooding, real estate being scooped up, and Jeff's death? Maybe I'm trying to put too much together, but this lake is normally quiet, and suddenly all kinds of things are happening, and they all center around one family."

"I never thought of any of those things being connected. I'd closed Jeff's case, and then Maggie was in here the other day with some new evidence she insisted be tested. She had a commuter cup she'd found in the vicinity of where the boat capsized that she said was Jeff's. She also had a cassette tape with someone's voice on it that she thought was suspicious. The tape belonged to Jeff too. Seemed he still relied on an old answering machine and the house phone. Anyway, I still haven't heard back on who the voice on the tape might be. It didn't sound like anyone from around here, but it sounded familiar."

Erin shuffled in her seat. "Do you still have it? I mean, could I hear it?"

The sheriff dug through drawers and came up with an envelope. He emptied the tiny cassette onto the cluttered desk, pulled the ancient cassette player out, and plugged it in. The tape inserted into the slot he hit play. "Nine o'clock, northwest corner of the dam."

"That's Rogers," Erin said. "Chief Engineer Rogers with the Corps of Engineers at the dam."

The sheriff rewound the tape and once more hit play. "Nine o'clock, northwest corner of the dam."

Erin leaned in toward the desk. "I just talked to him,

and he said he left a message for Jeff about meeting him at the dam. I'm sure that's his voice."

The sheriff flinched. "Rogers, from the dam? Chief Rogers with the Corps of Engineers. That's it. That's whose voice that is. I knew I recognized it. I sent it to Tulsa to be analyzed."

"I'm sure that is Chief Rogers, and he said he left a message for Jeff the night he died, and Jeff never showed for the meeting. He was planning to give Jeff a tour of the dam to prove its safety," she said.

The sheriff sat back in his seat and rubbed his jaw.

Erin cocked her head and looked at the sheriff wondering what was on his mind, but he showed no signs of speaking. "And what of the commuter cup? Did you get those contents analyzed?"

The sheriff stopped, once more reaching for his coffee cup. "Yes, I sent it in, but I don't have the results back yet."

Silence fell in the room as Erin thought over what she'd learned.

"Erin, this sheds some new light on this case. Thank you."

Erin nodded. "Can you let me know what you get back on those results?" Erin asked as she stood to leave.

"You bet," the sheriff said and rose to walk her out.

Chapter 25

Chris took off the jacket and tie he'd worn for the funeral. Too much, he thought. A shirt and trousers would be better. A minimalist, he had few clothes these days, and the only things here at his mom's house was what he left in his closet years ago. He didn't need much when he was on a shoot and didn't want to carry useless things. He was surprised Mom hadn't cleaned out his room and used it for something else. Maybe he should do that for her before he left. The baseball and bat from high school should go to someone who might use them. And the clothes? No one wanted those.

"You going somewhere?" Maggie looked him up and down as she stood at the stove stirring something.

"Yeah, dinner with Ryan in Tulsa. Don't wait up." He kissed his mother on the cheek and rushed out the back door before she could question him. He'd already asked to use Dad's car for the evening. It seemed less embarrassing than asking Mom. It was hard to go back home when you were an adult.

Climbing in the sedan he found his dad had cleaned out the normal chaos. The car needed to be vacuumed, but it wasn't too bad. He'd seen Ryan's car and knew it was always a mess. Interesting how an accountant could be so cluttered in her daily life. A place for everything and everything in its place was not true with Ryan.

She buzzed him in when he called her on the

security button at the bottom of the stairs to the apartment complex. And he was right. Not much had changed since she moved out of her parents' house and into a place of her own. It was clean, but papers lay on the couch and coffee table. Coffee cups sat in the kitchen sink.

"I'll be right out," she called from the bedroom.

He stood, hands in pockets, trying to decide where to sit when she walked down the hall into the living room in stiletto heels.

Her fiery red hair hung loose on her shoulders, and she wore an emerald-green dress that came to a deep V in front. A delicate silver chain fell between her breasts. He knew he'd be distracted by the dress all night until he could get her out of it—a thought he pushed down for later.

"You look great. I didn't know if I needed a jacket. Where are we going? You were taking care of the reservations."

"There's an Irish pub I thought you might like. I don't think we need reservations." She smiled and walked toward him looping her hand through the crook in his arm leading him out. She clicked the lock on the way out.

She was right. The restaurant was crowded but the wait for a table was not long. They both ordered a beer on tap, and it didn't take long for the crab cakes and Reuben rolls to appear.

"You look fantastic in that dress. Of course, you can rock anything you wear, but I love the dress."

Ryan smiled. "Thank you. I had you in mind when I pulled it out of the closet." She fingered the silver necklace.

"I only had one nice thing to wear, and I wore it to my uncle's funeral. The clothes in my old bedroom closet have been there a few years. I need something new. Or maybe I need to go back to work. Or just get an apartment and stay here. I can't decide."

"Well, don't let me sway you." She winked.

"Of course, you sway me. You always have. But seriously, I need to make a decision."

The waiter cleared the plates and brought another round of beer.

Ryan took a sip, set the glass down, and looked Chris in the eye. "Since we're being serious here, I had something to talk to you about."

"Ok," he said wondering what was so serious.

"Erin Sampson and I have been looking into the sale of real estate around the lake. You know how many of the lots have gone up for sale, people disappeared almost overnight, especially since the lake levels have been up and down."

Chris nodded his head.

"How well do you know your brother-in-law, Ted? I mean, I know he and Hope have been married a long time, but do you think he's a good guy?"

Chris raised his eyebrow and took a drink. "I don't know what you're getting at. I've known Ted Shipley since he and Hope were dating. I was just a kid and didn't pay too much attention. But once they were married, they had all those kids in a hurry. I think Hope is happy. I guess he's a good guy. I've never been around him much. I went off to college shortly after their wedding and then never really came home much after that. Why would you ask?"

"When Erin and I began to make a spreadsheet of all

the property being bought up around the lake after the flooding began, there was one name that kept coming up—T & H Realty, LLC."

"Who's T & H Realty, LLC?"

"Erin checked with the Secretary of State, and it turns out the company is owned by Ted and Hope Shipley, thus T & H." She looked at him over her glass.

"What? I don't think Ted and Hope have the money to own a bunch of land. I mean, I don't know how many properties you're talking about, but with five kids, they don't have a lot of disposable cash just lying around. They're normal people like us. Hope doesn't work outside the home, she's busy with the kids, and with only one income, I don't see how they could."

"Rumor is that he is overextended. I talked to someone at the bank who will remain nameless. It would take a court order to find out for sure, but it seems unusual that the flooding began just as all the property started to change hands, don't you think?"

"You think Shipley has a hand in this. And if he did, why do you think real estate sales are sinister?" He tossed his napkin on the table and leaned back. "How many properties are we talking about?"

"You don't believe me."

"I want to, but this is my sister and brother-in-law we're talking about. I can't imagine my big sister involved in a real estate scam. That's what you're saying, aren't you?" Chris could feel the heat on his face as he spoke.

"Now don't get excited. I just asked a question."

"No, you accused. Is that what this date is all about? Were you just trying to get information out of me?"

"No! I wanted to see you. And I wanted to know

what you thought."

"I think you're on the wrong path. I know my sister would never cheat her neighbors, if she had the money, and she doesn't. How many properties are you talking about anyway?"

"Several."

He stared at her closely.

Her eyes blazed, and she huffed. "You don't believe me. Okay, big guy, let's go to my office. I'll show you the spreadsheet." Ryan stood.

Chris paused, took a long draw on his beer, then threw some bills on the table and followed her out the door. This had better be good, he thought.

In the empty accounting building Chris stood looking over Ryan's shoulder. After hours, the only light that shone was her office and the hallway leading to it.

"See these columns list all the owners—both past and present. And here"—she opened another window on the screen—"are copies of each of the deeds converting ownership to T & H Realty, LLC." She stood and offered Chris her chair. He sat then scrolled through the scanned deeds on the screen—and she was right. It showed property conveyed from the former owners to the present ones. And all of the present owners were T & H Realty, LLC.

He sat back in the chair and looked at Ryan. "I don't believe it. But like I said, maybe he did it to help his neighbors, not cheat them." He rubbed his head.

"You don't believe it? Erin and I worked long and hard trying to make sense of this and hoping to find that someone else was the owner of the property now. Like T & H had been a middleman or something. But that didn't happen. There have been no owners since T & H took possession. They are the present owners of most of the property around the lake in the area of the island where the rivers converge."

Chris shook his head.

"Are you still mad at me?" Ryan reached out a hand, and he took it.

"No, not mad, just amazed, I guess. I can't imagine my sister involved in this."

"Maybe she's not. Maybe Ted is pulling a fast one on everyone, including his wife." Ryan paused. "I've got more beer at the apartment," she said as she pulled him to his feet.

"I could use another," Chris said.

Ryan switched off her computer, and they left the office flipping off the lights as they went.

Chris followed her down the hallway to the back door where the car sat. He didn't know what to think. But he knew one thing—he really needed to talk to Erin about this. After that, he didn't know who he should talk to.

Eventually, he'd have to have a conversation with Hope.

Chapter 26

Chris pulled into the parking lot of Cronkite and Associates in the car he borrowed from Dad—again. The old building in downtown Tulsa looked stark: tall, brick, and unassuming in comparison to the modern ones. No glass or steel, it came from another era. But after opening the door and climbing the steps to the top, he found another glass door with ornate black and gold letters stating the name of the firm. Erin had set herself up nicely, he thought.

"I don't have an appointment but wanted to see Erin Sampson if she's available." He knew he should have called first. Still, it was hard to think of the little girl he used to swim with as an attorney in a prestigious law firm in downtown Tulsa.

"Let me check," the receptionist said after asking his name. She spoke quietly to someone on the other end. "She'll be right out," the receptionist said and instantly answered another call.

Chris sat down in the leather chair near the door and picked up a magazine. He'd barely found something to read when Erin walked into the waiting room in a skirt and blouse with the sleeves rolled up like she'd been working. And looking very grown up.

"Chris," Erin said in surprise. "I was shocked when Anna said you were here. What can I do for you?" She smiled as she walked forward with her hand extended.

He stood and shook her hand. "I hope I'm not intruding. I should have called first, but I wanted to talk to you about real estate on the lake. I had a conversation the other night with Ryan, and she said the two of you were working together on something."

She relaxed. "Of course. Come on back to my office."

Chris followed her down the long hallway lined with offices and attorneys on the phone and working at their desks. Some doors were closed, but it was obvious that most of the offices were beautifully furnished. They rounded the corner, and Erin escorted him into a small office with a window that looked into the alley behind the building. Two small chairs sat in front of a desk.

"Welcome to my tiny office. I'm an associate, and so I get the leftovers, but I love working here and hope to move up someday." She gestured that he should take a seat.

"Not so bad. It looks pretty good for a new attorney. It's a big firm, and I'm sure they're happy to have you." Chris looked around. "I'm used to sitting on a rock waiting for just the right light to take a shot. This is nice."

"My aunt is a partner, and she got me a job here while I was in college. I did grunt work while in school, and then after law school and passing the bar, they offered me a fulltime job as an associate attorney. I'm very lucky."

"It looks that way, and I'm sure you work hard. But I talked to Ryan the other night, and she mentioned the two of you had put together some properties that had been purchased by T & H Realty."

"Yes, Ryan and I hadn't seen each other for years since school, and then our paths crossed. I guess the bank had noticed what they thought were too many parcels of land changing hands and asked her firm to look into it. Our law firm represents the Sunset Hills Homeowners' Association, and they too were concerned about all the sales. So, we ended up working on this project together. When I arrived at Ryan's office, she already had the deeds and found the common denominator."

"Yes, she mentioned T & H Realty. She also said that was owned by Ted and Hope Shipley—my sister and her husband."

Erin sat up straight in her chair and cleared her throat. "It took some digging, but the LLC is owned by Ted and Hope. We found the documents registered with the Secretary of State, and they list their home address as the address of the LLC."

"I was hoping there was a mistake. I can't believe Hope is a part of this."

Erin had been fiddling with a pencil and put it down. "Chris, there's nothing illegal about owning property."

"But where did they get the money?"

"I heard through a source I can't name that the bank has cut him off. He's borrowed too much and can't have more until he begins to show a profit. He also applied for a loan for a boat. I think that was the final straw for the bank."

Chris slid back in his seat. "To buy a boat? Locally?"

"Yes, at the marina where they moor the yachts, I think. I thought that was strange. I mean why would Ted need a yacht? He fished with Jeff sometimes, and they do have five children, so they'd need a big boat. But maybe a pontoon."

Chris rubbed his chin thinking. "And why buy

property that is flooded all the time? You and I know that lake and know what the land is like underneath all that water. We've seen it. But right now, with all the rains and runoff, it's flooded. So why buy it?"

"Because it's cheap when it's flooded? Like you said, sometimes it isn't flooded. On a regular year, it's dry land. Maybe it's a smart business deal. But the problem is that so much of that land just sold overnight without any advertising for sale or whatever. I guess as a realtor, Ted might know who all wanted to sell their property and so he bought it up hoping for a dryer year. Or maybe he was trying to help out his neighbors in a time of need. I don't know."

Chris looked out the window with the telephone pole in the middle and then back at Erin. "But did Hope know? I mean she'd have to, wouldn't she?"

"I would think so, but I don't know how they run their home life."

Chris looked off in thought and then back. "I guess I need to talk to my sister."

He fiddled with some lint on his jeans. "You know land sales aren't the only problem. The dam is old and under a lot of pressure right now with the rains. You knew I was going to accompany Rogers from the Corps of Engineers on a scuba diving trip to the dam. We checked the outside of the dam intakes and found them to be horribly clogged with zebra mussels. I've never seen such an infestation. It was odd to us that they aren't that bad on our dock and my dad's boat motor. I mean, they are everywhere on the lake, but not that many in one place. It seemed odd. The water is always moving through those intakes but yet they managed to multiply to that degree. I wonder if they had some help. You know—were they placed there? Who would do that and why? Everyone around here depends on that dam. Why mess it up to the point it is not working?"

"It doesn't make sense. And the rains this summer have been relentless so the stress on the dam has been worse," Erin said.

Chris once again looked out the window. "So, who would benefit from clogging up the dam on a year when releasing the water at a rapid rate is needed more than ever?" He shook his head.

Erin stared directly into his eyes. "I see a lot of bad stuff in this job, and I try to not get jaded, but to answer your question, the person who would benefit from more flooding would be the person who is buying up land that is flooded—at cheap prices. Land that would be dry on a regular year and sell for a much higher price."

The room grew quiet, and Chris rubbed his head in thought. "I'm sorry to take up your day like this. Thank you for taking the time to talk to me." He stood.

Erin rose from her desk. "Anytime. You are always welcome and let me know if I can do anything for you and your family. We've been friends for a long time." She held out her hand and he took it, then walked back out the door toward what he hoped was the waiting room.

Chapter 27

Chris and Hope sat on the bench swing. They rocked as they watched her children frolic on the playground equipment. Baby Sara lay in her arms. The lacy sun and shade moved in time with their swing. It was enough to make him sleepy too. The last time he'd spent this much time with his sister her oldest twins were the age of the one dozing in the sun with a bottle hanging from her mouth. Kids were amazing. He didn't know if he wanted any of his own. He'd have to change his lifestyle if he were to do that, but he still loved to watch hers. The squeals of laughter made him smile.

"They're great, Hope. I know I haven't been around much in the last few years, but your kids are incredible."

"Makes you want some of your own, huh?" Hope brushed the hair from the face of the sleeping child.

"I don't know about that. You do a good job at this parenting thing. Maybe you should be the one in charge of procreation."

"Well, I've done a good job of having them. I never planned to have five. The first set was an accident way too early in our marriage, and then it just took off from there. When you have them two at a time, the house fills up fast."

"Like I said, they're great." Chris stared across the park deep in thought trying to decide how to bring up the conversation about T & H Realty, LLC. They sat in silence.

"It's too bad it took a funeral to get me home. But I'm glad I came." He paused trying to think of a way to bring up the subject of the realty company. "You know, one of the things that Uncle Jeff had in his billfold was a business card." Chris glanced at his sister.

She shrugged. "I don't think I saw any of that. I was too busy with the kids and trying to keep Mom on her feet."

"Yeah, you had your work cut out for you. But Mom, Dad, and I looked at the items once the sheriff brought them to the house, and he had a card for T & H Realty, LLC. Do you know who that is?"

"No, I don't think so. It can't be local, or I'd have heard of it."

"You know Ryan's firm has been looking into the sale of property around the lake. Erin Sampson has also. They've been working on it together. Ryan created a spreadsheet with all the properties around the lake that have sold in the last year and one name kept coming up, T & H Realty, LLC."

Hope turned and looked at him. "The same as the card in Uncle Jeff's billfold? I still have no idea who owns that. Have you looked into it? I mean if it's important."

Jenny or Jill (he could never keep them straight) ran to her mother giggling.

"Mommy, Emory is pretending to be a bug. Watch him!" She ran back to the playground where here brothers and sister played. The older boy crawled along the edge of the barrier to the park on all fours with his eyes bugging out.

"Cute. Kids have such imaginations," Chris said as

he watched from the sidelines. He cleared his throat. "Back to the card. Ryan and Erin looked into who owns T & H Realty, LLC. They looked at deeds to the properties—and there are several." He took a deep breath. "And T & H Realty, LLC is Ted and Hope Shipley." He again glanced at his sister. She sat holding the baby and smiled at the oldest boy, waving with one hand. Then she lowered her hand and twisted toward him. "What? That can't be right. I'm sure I'd know if there was another Ted and Hope Shipley in town, or even in Tulsa."

Chris felt his body grow cold. How could he explain this to her? "No, I don't think there is. You and Ted own that property, well the company does. I thought there was a mistake too, but there doesn't seem to be. The deeds all say T & H Realty, LLC and Ted's signature line shows him as CEO of the company. I assumed you knew."

She stiffened. "Ted is a realtor. He helps people buy and sell property all the time, but the only real estate we own is the house we live in. And even that mortgage is hard to pay sometimes. That's a mistake." She stood with the baby in arms and her mouth set in a determined way. "And I need to get the kids in. I have to start supper soon."

"I'm sorry. I didn't mean to be the bearer of bad news. I just wondered what you knew about this."

"I know I don't own a bunch of lake property. Your friends are mistaken." She called the children to her as she walked to the van and placed the baby in the seat.

Chris helped get the children in their car seats listening to them complain about heading home on a warm spring day and again marveled at how calm his sister stayed. She was born to be a mother. But maybe she wasn't born to be a businessperson. He wondered how much Ted slipped by Hope on a daily basis.

Maybe he needed to talk to Dad. He always had his finger on the pulse of the community.

Chapter 28

Saturday morning came early for Chris as usual. He didn't sleep well anymore. It was understandable being up at all hours for the perfect lighting on a shoot. But since he came home to his parents, he still felt uneasy in his own bedroom where he grew up. Maybe because he was a grownup and felt he'd outgrown the place. Mom and Dad were gracious and had not yet asked him when he planned to go back to work.

He sat at the kitchen table mulling over the conversations he'd had with Ryan and Erin and decided as soon as Dad was up, he'd ask him to go fishing. Once they were alone, he could broach the subject of T & H Realty.

Mom walked in first with Dad right behind her laughing. Chris had no idea what was funny, but they made a great couple. Even though Dad was gone a lot, they seemed to make up for lost time on the weekends.

"Morning," he said smiling. "What's so funny?" He gestured to the almost full coffee pot so they would know it was available.

Maggie tied her bathrobe. "We were laughing about the coffee being ready when we got up. It's like butler service having you here."

"I'm never without my coffee if possible."

Maggie poured two cups and sat at the table with one. "I always wondered how you had your morning coffee in the middle of nowhere."

"It's instant and not very good. But I can heat water with a fire or solar powered stove. I get my caffeine somehow."

Dad sat down looking scruffy without a shave, robe hanging open, sipping from his cup.

Chris looked at him thinking he had aged since he last really looked at him. "I was thinking, we still haven't been fishing together since I got here. I need to go back to work soon, and I'd love to take the boat out for a spin. What do you say? Do you have any plans this morning?"

Dad looked at Mom and raised one eyebrow. "Do we?"

"No, you boys go fishing. Let me fix some breakfast, and I'll pack a quick lunch. I think you should. It's been a while for both of you."

Full of breakfast and with Maggie's lunch packed in an ice chest they pulled the boat away from the dock. Chris had made sure the night before it was gassed up and ready to go. A day of fishing with Dad reminded him of his youth. He was lucky to grow up on a lake with a father who took an interest in his children. Chris was aware not all fathers were as present as his had been. It wasn't until after he and Hope left home that Dad began to travel with his job. Chris only assumed that it made better money, or he probably wouldn't do it.

The morning sun reflected off the still water as they glided across the lake to a place they used to fish when Chris was young. His dad at the helm, Chris watched him maneuver the boat he'd owned for years.

His dad surveyed the water and slowed the speed of the boat, then stopped, looking out into the water, leaving his craft to drift. "I can't believe how good you have this boat looking. It's been neglected lately."

"It just needed a little t.l.c., and I was home to do it."

"I can't tell you how much I appreciate it." Dad walked to the back of the boat to toss the anchor over and then reached for a pole. "There's plenty of artificial bait in my tackle box since we don't have anything live."

Chris picked up the extra pole and then dug through the tackle box. He had no idea what the bass were hitting on right now, but there were several spinner lures he could use. He threaded one on the line he pulled from the end of the pole and glanced up at his dad who already had a hook in the water.

"So, what's up with you and Ryan?" Dad asked over his shoulder. "I noticed you were in the kitchen raiding the fridge the other night like you used to in high school after sneaking out of your room. So, I know something's up."

Chris felt himself blush and was glad Dad's back was to him. "You knew about that, huh? That was a long time ago." Chris cast his line into the water.

"Yeah, I knew about it. She's a great girl. Your mom and I have always liked her. We were surprised when you broke up in college."

"That was my idea. I think I panicked at the idea of settling down, and it really upset her. She married less than a year later to some duffus she met on the rebound. I guess that didn't last too long. She heard about Uncle Jeff's death. I guess the whole town knew—you can't keep a secret in Mannford. But she called me about the time of the funeral, and we met up again. It's been great. Well, most of it has been great."

"Most of it?" Dad still had his back to his son. Chris and his father had often communicated this way while fishing. It seemed normal to them even if it might not have been to others.

"We went out to dinner the other night when I borrowed your car. Thanks again for that. I feel like a kid when I have to ask to borrow the car. But we went out to dinner, and she dropped a bombshell on me."

"I'm not about to become a grandfather again, am I?" Paul paused. "I guess you haven't been home long enough for that. Have you?"

Chris laughed. "No, not that type of bombshell. But what she told me is what I wanted to talk to you about today."

"I thought you might have had ulterior motives."

Chris cleared his throat. "It seems that Ryan and Erin Sampson have teamed up to look at sales of property around this lake. As you know, many of the lots have sold lately, and most of them are underwater."

"Yes, your mom and I have discussed how many of our neighbors have just up and left. We guessed because of the flooding."

Chris reeled in and recast in another section of water near the boat. It would have been nice to catch a fish even if that weren't the reason for the trip. "Probably so. But it seems that most all the land that has traded hands lately is located in one place and ended up being bought by T & H Realty here in Mannford. Ever heard of it?"

"Yes, lately. There was a business card in Jeff's billfold for T & H Realty."

Nothing hit on Chris' line, so he once again reeled in. He paused. "Erin dug into T & H Realty." He glanced back at his dad. "It took some looking but found it belonged to Ted and Hope Shipley."

There was silence from the other side of the boat.

"Ted and Hope? Our Ted and Hope?"

"The business address was their home."

Chris could hear his dad turn toward him as he reeled in his line.

"There must be some mistake in her research. Our Ted and Hope can barely pay their own mortgage sometimes. I mean, Hope has mentioned how tight things are with his salary based on sales, and she doesn't work."

Chris paused. "And there's more. Ted has been looking at yachts. I know again from Erin who has contacts at the bank. I can't imagine why he'd need or even want a yacht unless he was trying to impress the customers—maybe take them out to see the lake to get them to buy real estate."

"They sure can't afford a yacht," Paul said.

Chris looked at his father on the other side of the boat and tried to think of how to say what he had to say. "I know. I wonder if Hope knows about the LLC. I mean, he could have set it up without her knowledge. Do you think Ted would do that? I mean you know him better than I do."

The men stared at each other across the boat. Chris' pole stood upright as water ran down and dripped onto his deck shoes. Paul opened his mouth to say something and then closed it. He shook his head.

"I don't know," he said. "But let's not bring this up to your mom right now. Let's see what we can find out and keep it between us."

"Agreed," Chris said and reached in the cooler for a bottle of water handing one to Dad.

Chapter 29

"Sheriff, the lab in Tulsa is on the line," the part time receptionist at the sheriff's office called from her desk. The small town had little to do most of the time and so only a part time receptionist was needed. Mondays were always busy after the weekend, and things slowed to a crawl until Friday when people got crazy again. Maybe they were tired of the workweek and just needed to blow off steam, but the weekend normally got busy at the sheriff's office.

He nodded back at her.

"Sheriff Montgomery," he said into the aging phone system. It still worked, and that was good because the county didn't have money to replace it.

The voice of the lab tech on the other end cleared his throat. "Sheriff, we analyzed the contents of the cup you sent us. Even though it's been sitting around for a while, it's obvious it's mostly bourbon, but with enough copper—probably from a copper-based algaecide—to poison and kill an adult male. I hope that's what you wanted to hear."

The sheriff rubbed his head. This was not the news he wanted to hear. Now he'd have to deal with Maggie. "Not really. But you think there was enough of the copper to kill him, huh? The liquid in the commuter cup was poison. I mean, could it have been an accident?"

"I don't see how. The deliberate ingestion of copper for suicidal purposes in humans has been reported.

Accidental ingestion has occurred through food or water that has been contained in copper vessels. So that could be what happened. But according to what I've found, early signs and symptoms of copper poisoning include a metallic taste, nausea, vomiting, and abdominal pain. And it would happen in a hurry with this much copper algaecide."

"So, if he was already drinking and was hit with the stomach issues from the algaecide, he could have fallen out of the boat and drowned."

"I guess. It would have been very painful," the lab tech on the other end responded. "Is there anything else you need at this time?"

"No, not really. Thank you for your help. Oh, you'll fax over the printed report like always." It wasn't really a question, it was the way they did things, first a verbal report and then the printed one. The sheriff hung up the phone and stared off into space. He'd have to tell Maggie what he found out. Chances were good Jeff was murdered. He doubted the man committed suicide and, if he had, there were easier ways to go. A bottle of sleeping pills downed with bourbon would be a lot less painful.

It was almost 5:00, and that meant Maggie would be home soon. He might as well go talk to her now, then he could call it a night.

Sheriff Montgomery stood at the back door on the deck about to knock when he heard someone behind him.

"Sheriff." Chris came up the path from the dock. Maggie and Paul's son had been home for a few weeks since his uncle's passing.

"Hey, Chris. How are you? I came to see your mom, is she home yet?"

As if on cue, Maggie's compact car pulled into the driveway, and she stepped out waving as she walked to the house.

"Sheriff, what brings you here? I hope it is good news."

"I do have some news, but I don't know if it's good or not. I would guess not."

Maggie looked him up and down and sighed. "Come in, Sheriff, I'll put on some coffee."

"Thanks, but that won't be necessary. I was on my way home. But I came to tell you I got the contents of the commuter cup analyzed, and it came back with copper poisoning. It is probably from a copper-based algaecide that's being used around the lake to kill the zebra mussels."

Maggie's face drained of color, and she reached for the railing built around the deck.

"Mom, let's sit down," Chris said, taking his mother's arm and guiding her to the patio table.

"I knew it," she said, sitting in the chair Chris held for her. "I don't know why I reacted that way, I knew he didn't just drown. But how did it get in his cup? I mean who would have put it there?" Then after a moment's silence, "I'm sure he didn't do it himself. I mean, Jeff had problems, but he wasn't suicidal. If he had been, he would have done that right after his wife died."

The water in the lake lapped the dock. It was the only sound heard as the people on the deck were silent.

The sheriff shook his head. "I knew Jeff most of my life, and I never thought he'd commit suicide. I guess you just never know. But if it wasn't suicide or an accident, who would want to hurt him?"

Chris cleared his throat. "Sheriff, when the guy from

the Corps of Engineers and I checked out the dam the other day, we found a lot of zebra mussels. I know that's not news to anyone at the lake. But I talked to a biologist who is working on the zebra mussel problem with the Corps. He said his lab was broken into recently and the mussels they planned on experimenting with, disappeared. They were going to use the copper-based algaecides to see how well it killed the invasive species. No one reported the break in because it didn't seem like much of a crime. But whoever took the mussels had access to the copper. Although I guess you can buy it anywhere."

Sheriff Montgomery's eyes narrowed. "A break in is a break in, no matter what was taken. They should have reported it. I'll go talk to them."

The patio was silent again, the waves lapping in the distance. "Oh, Sheriff," Maggie said, "I found Jeff's notebook. He kept records of when he fished and where and who he was with. I don't know why. He was just meticulous about his fishing and love of the lake. Would you like to see it?"

"Yes. Maybe it might shed some light on this."

Maggie nodded and headed for the kitchen, then returned quickly.

She flipped open the notebook and showed it to the sheriff. "See, he always dated the entries. Here he says he was going to the dam to meet Ted and to see why the dam was clogged up and talk to the Corps of Engineers. I know he confided in Ted about his findings, and they were going to the dam to talk with the engineer who worked there. In fact, he was going to meet Ted the night he died."

Sheriff Montgomery noticed Chris flinch before

leaning in to read the notebook over his shoulder.

"Maggie, do you mind if I keep this for a while? I'll get it back to you," the sheriff said flipping it closed.

"No, of course not, if it will help. You can have anything you need."

Sheriff Montgomery glanced toward the cruiser. "I've taken up enough of your time. But I promise to let you know as soon as I hear anything. Try to get some rest and let me know if you think of anything else."

"Thank you, Sheriff." Maggie stepped back, and the officer walked off the deck.

"Good, night, Sheriff," Chris said and headed for the back door.

Montgomery thought he'd call Erin on his way home and let her know what he found out about the contents of the cup. And should he be concerned about Ted Shipley's meeting with Jeff?

Chapter 30

The Corps of Engineers' lab was immaculate. The gleaming white tile walls and stainless-steel tables were almost too bright to look at. Fluorescent lights hung above each table, and scientists in white lab coats and latex gloves looked up when the sheriff walked in with the head biologist.

"As you can see, we have a small lab, and everyone wears gloves while they work. We even ask the cleaning crew to wear gloves to avoid contamination. They come in after hours when we've all gone home. I've had the same cleaning crew for years and trust each and every one of them. I am sure they had nothing to do with the break in."

"Of course," said Sheriff Montgomery. "I didn't mean to implicate anyone from your office. I'm sure they are all above board. But you should have reported the break in."

"The only thing taken was a bucket of crustaceans, so I really didn't think it was important. It was more trouble than it was worth. I know you have other things to do, Sheriff."

"We have a problem at the moment and need to have the crime lab out here to fingerprint the lab. Is that okay? I mean if all your people wear gloves, then there won't be much to find. They should be here any time."

Sheriff Montgomery stepped from the lab and wrote

in his notebook as he called the office. He hoped the crime lab was on the way, but he'd check. The receptionist assured him she had called them, and then he saw the van rounding the corner to the parking lot of the lab. They pulled to the front door, and several officers climbed out pulling on coveralls and heading to the door.

The head biologist gave his workers the afternoon off, and the sheriff stepped out of the way as the crime lab went to work checking surfaces and asking where the specimens had been kept. They worked as one unit, and the sheriff was amazed at the things they looked at. He could use some time following them around in hopes he could learn a thing or two.

The criminologist who the sheriff had spoken with earlier walked over to him as the others headed out the door. "Sheriff, we'll take this evidence back to our lab and see what we find, and we'll be in touch." The crime lab left as quickly as they came, and the sheriff went back to his office to await their reports. It might be interesting to see what they came up with. If the fingerprints didn't belong to the Corps, who did they belong to?

****

The more Erin thought about it the more she knew she needed to meet the man who worked the night shift at the dam. She knew Rob was working late tonight, so maybe when she got off work she'd go by the dam.

She left the office later than normal and ran by the apartment to change her clothes and then drove to the dam. Parking in the lot she walked down the steps where fishermen stood with poles in the water.

She smiled as she walked past one after another who cast after she walked past or reeled in the line to move to another spot.

Down near the end of the walkway an old man stood bent over his tackle box. He grumbled to himself as he leaned down. She thought he looked familiar.

"Catch anything?" she asked. He looked up, and she was certain he was the man she met on the deck at Jeff's funeral. Allen something.

He looked surprised that she had spoken to him or maybe he recognized her, then he smiled.

"Evening, miss," he said and finished standing up to his full height.

"Evening," Erin said and stuck her hand out in greeting. "Erin Sampson. I think we met at Jeff Larson's funeral. I'm a friend of Chris'."

"Of course. I thought you looked familiar. Allen White's my name."

"I remembered the Allen part but couldn't come up with a last name. You're a neighbor of the Becks."

"Yep, we've been neighbors for years. My wife and I watched their kids grow up."

Erin smiled. "I used to swim with them when I was a kid, so I was probably in the middle of all those kids part of the time. I'm originally from Mannford but work in Tulsa now."

Allen fingered the hook untwisting it and hooking it in the loop on the rod. "Yeah, Mannford has lost a lot of its citizens over the years to Tulsa and the big cities. I understand, people gotta work and if there's nowhere to do that, they move on. But it's a shame."

"Yes, it is. I love my job in Tulsa, but I'm drawn to this lake and find myself here more all the time. The big city can be a drain, and the water is like therapy."

Snapping the tackle box closed, Allen stood again groaning. "Well, if they don't do something about this dam soon, we won't have a lake to come to. The wife and I moved here when we were young and lived here most of our lives, but it seems like the fish aren't biting anymore. Probably because of the chemicals they put in the water to get rid of those zebra mussels. And now the water is just trickling out of the spillway. I know for a fact that it runs better in the daytime than in the night—all the night fishermen do. That guy who takes care of the dam at night, I thinking he's sleeping on the job. I see him go in there, but then the water just seems to slow down. I don't think it is just a coincidence that it flows out heavier during the day when everyone can see it than it does at night, do you?" Allen looked at Erin and squinted his eyes into the evening sun. "It was nice to meet you again. I think I'll go on home and have a TV dinner. No fish tonight."

"Nice to meet you again too, Allen. Have a good evening."

She watched him slowly make his way up the stairs to where she was sure his pickup sat awaiting his return. She leaned against the railing that kept her and many others from falling into the river that ran downstream to Tulsa. She took a sip from the commuter cup that held the afternoon tea from the office. It tasted terrible, but she swallowed—and then thought of the cup that Jeff might have taken his last drink from. She unscrewed her lid pouring out the liquid into the water below. Why was the water coming out more slowly at night? The Corps of Engineers assured her it was being discharged at a normal rate. It sprayed from the outflow release valves as the sun sparkled off the water. What did it look like after dark?

She climbed back up the steps to her car and crawled

in wondering about the lake she'd grown up on. She'd wait and see if the night employee came to work. Maybe she'd get a chance to talk to him. Almost dozing in the waning sunshine, she was startled by a door slamming at the end of the parking lot. A man in a gray uniform walked away from his pickup and up the stairs that led to the top of the concrete dam. The same stairs Rogers had taken her up when she toured with him. Was he the night shift she wondered? Maybe she should find out. He opened the door with a key and stepped inside as the sun set behind the behemoth concrete structure. Darkness was falling quickly.

Erin stepped out of her car and looked at the water as it rushed out of the spillway and into the river below. Slowly lights came on in the parking lot highlighting her car, and she realized she was alone in the parking lot. Not even a night fisherman was set up to fish from the spillway, when suddenly the noise of the water became less deafening. Like a faucet being turned off and the water began to slow its flow from the dam. Had he slowed the water discharge?

It was time to talk to the night shift she thought as she climbed the steps to the top of the dam and knocked on the door. It took several times of rapping her knuckles on the door before someone opened it. A short man stood in the doorway and looked her up and down.

"Dam's closed, ma'am. Sorry." He started to close the door.

"Hi. I'm Erin Sampson." Her heart raced as she thought of the fact she was alone in the dark with this stranger whose name tag said "Decker." And she was getting some strange vibes off him.

"Nice to meet you, but like I said the dam is closed."

"Oh, okay. I heard that someone took care of the dam at night. I won't keep you, but I'm an attorney for the Sunset Hills Homeowners' Association and I just had a couple of questions, Mr. Decker." She nodded to his name badge.

"Like I said, we're closed. Talk to Rogers during the day."

"I did, and he said that the water ran at the same rate day and night. And I just saw it slow to a trickle. Can you tell me why that is? Also, why does the dam have an overabundance of zebra mussels? The scuba divers saw a lot of mussels clogging up the intake valves when they were down there. They said more than what was on their boat motors and docks."

His face contorted in the small amount of light that spilled from the doorway, and he drew a deep breath. Then slammed the door.

"We're closed!" he shouted from behind the metal door.

Chapter 31

Erin wondered what Maggie might know about the real estate sales around the lake. She knew everyone and everything going on in her hometown. The short time they spoke after the funeral wasn't the time to bring up the problems with the lake. And after the confrontation with Decker at the dam, she had more questions. Maybe it was time for a trip to Maggie's and see if she knew something Erin didn't.

She pulled into the gravel driveway of Maggie's house and realized she had company. A blue sedan sat where Paul normally parked when he was home. About to back out and come back at a more convenient time, she saw Maggie stand from the table that sat on the deck. Too late, she'd been spotted.

Erin put the car back in park and climbed out. Maggie walked toward her with a glass in hand and waved when she saw who exited the vehicle.

"Erin! To what do I owe this surprise?" Maggie walked down the steps toward Erin's car.

"I was about to leave when I saw you had company. I don't want to intrude. Maybe I should have called first."

Maggie patted Erin's shoulder her with her free hand. "Nonsense," she said and gestured to the deck. "My friend Allison and I were having a glass of tea. Please join us."

"Well, I won't take long."

Maggie stepped to the table and pulled out a chair for her. "You remember Allison Wells? I'll get you some tea. Sugar? "

"That would be wonderful. And yes, of course I remember Allison," Erin said. "It's been a while. How are you?" She nodded to the woman who sat drinking tea with her back to the cove.

Allison took a sip and looked closely at Erin. "Erin Sampson, right? How's your mother?"

"Oh, Mom's fine. Still working too many hours, and I don't see her as much as I used to when I lived here. But we still get together as often as possible."

Maggie returned quickly and placed Erin's tea glass in front of her, then sat. "So, what brings you back to Mannford?"

Erin took a sip of the tea. It reminded her of her mother's—fresh brewed. No instant here. "I represent the Sunset Hills Homeowners' Association, and they are concerned for the property values around the lake. I was certain you knew everyone, and I thought you might be able to shed some light on the subject."

"We've been around here a long time. What do you want to know?"

Erin cleared her throat. "First of all, again let me say how sorry I am about Jeff. His death was such a surprise to everyone around here."

"Thank you. Allison and I were just talking about that. The Sheriff—and everyone else, I guess—just wrote it off as an accident by a drunk who should have known better, but lately more evidence has surfaced that it might have been murder. I found Jeff's commuter cup and took it to the sheriff. There was poison in the cup that belonged to Jeff."

"Yes, I spoke with Sheriff Montgomery. I suppose there are no suspects yet."

Maggie wiped away the moisture from the patio table with her hand. "No. No suspects. I just can't believe anyone would do that to Jeff. Everyone loved him. Yes, he had an angry streak when he was drinking, but murder?" Tears shone in her eyes.

Erin reached for her hand and grasped it, then spoke. "I know. It is very hard to think of anyone deliberately hurting someone you love."

Voices could be heard in the distance as men laughed and walked up the drive.

"Maggie, you there?"

Erin knew that voice, but she was unsure from where.

"On the deck, Allen." She stood as Allen White walked up the steps with a bowl in his hand. With him was Ralph Larson, Bernadette's father. She seldom saw Ralph anymore since moving to Tulsa. They'd recently seen each other when Erin sought him out before the townhall meeting.

"Hi, we didn't know there was a party." Allen smiled as he plopped down the bowl on the table. It smelled of fish.

"Ralph and me caught a mess of fish today. More than normal lately. I don't know what the difference was, but they was bitin'. Here. I brought you and Paul some fillets for supper."

Ralph put his arm around Erin. "Hi, kid. Good to see you again."

Maggie stood. "We were just talking about the health of the lake and you two bring us its bounty. Thank you. I'll put these in the fridge. Would you like to join us for tea?"

"No thank you, ma'am. We're dirty and smell like fish. At least I do, I can't speak for Ralph."

"I'm sure I do too." Ralph nodded as he spoke.

Maggie picked up the bowl. "So where did you fish today? Or is that a fisherman's secret?"

"Not by the dam, I can tell you. All the chemicals that have been dumped into the water by the dam have either run off or killed the fish. The corps says they were trying to get rid of the zebra mussels, but they got rid of the fish in the bargain."

"What are they dumping into the water?" Erin asked.

"A copper-based algaecide meant to kill off the mussels, but it seemed to deter the fish too," Ralph said. "So, we went to the other side of the lake. The fishing was great today. Maybe that was just luck, but we caught our limit."

Erin sat silent. Copper-based algaecide was what the sheriff said was in the commuter cup. Was Jeff poisoned with the same thing that was poisoning the lake? She decided to remain silent until she could talk to Montgomery again. No need to upset Maggie anymore. She'd been through enough.

"So, how's Bernadette, Ralph? I haven't spoken to her this week. I guess her designs are selling. I hope she's not spending all her time on my wedding dress."

"She's well. Getting ready for the birth of that baby and working. Her mom helps out a lot."

"Tell her I said hello and we need to get together soon." Erin felt a pang of guilt over how long it had been since she'd seen her friend. When they were in school they saw each other every day. Work and Rob kept her busy, and she tried to see her mom as often as possible. But she'd call her as soon as she got out of here, just to hear her voice.

Allison took another sip of tea and then set the glass back on the table. "The lake might improve as soon as they let enough water out. Levels seem to be getting lower, but there is still rain in the forecast. That dam can't take much more strain, zebra mussels or no."

They all nodded in agreement.

"We'll let you ladies enjoy that tea, and I hope you and Paul like the fish." Allen turned and headed back down the pathway that led to his home with Ralph in tow.

"Maggie, thank you for the tea. I didn't mean to intrude, but I need to get back home. Who knows what Rob might cook up in the kitchen left unattended." She stood to take the glass back into the kitchen, but Maggie took it from her hands.

"That's fine, dear, I've got it. You come and visit anytime and bring Rob with you."

The men were moving away down the steps as Erin reached her car thinking about copper-based algaecide.

Chapter 32

Erin clicked on the contact for her best friend, hit the speaker, then listened to it ring. She picked up the third time.

"Hey, lady. I was in the bathroom. Three months along, I'm hardly showing, and I'm constantly in the bathroom. Mom said I sat on her bladder for the whole nine months. I hope this little one doesn't. But how are you?"

Erin smiled as Bernadette rattled on. "I'm good. Just saw your dad, and it's been ages since we talked. I told him I'd call you. I just wanted to see how you were doing."

"I'm great. Getting big and can't stay out of the bathroom, but oh, I have a line on some silk for your dress and some *peau de soie* in rayon or silk for the lining, then of course Leavers lace for the overlay."

"Whoa, I don't even know what that means, but I hear dollar signs in your voice. I'll wear this dress for a few hours. It's not like it will be worn every day, and I have to pay caterers, florists, not to mention rental for the church…"

"I know, I just want it perfect. Maybe we can go by some fabric shops in Tulsa someday soon and look at cloth. But remember it will be a Larson original and could be handed down to that little girl you will have some day."

"Or yours," Erin teased. "If I have kids, they'll probably be ornery little boys with bugs and dirt all over them like their dad."

Bernadette laughed. It was good to hear her laugh. She hadn't done a lot of that lately since she found she was pregnant, and the father bailed on her. Erin still found that hard to believe. She kept thinking he'd see that cute, pink bundle of joy and melt like everyone else. But he'd left town so who knew.

"Where did you see Dad?" Bernadette asked.

"I was at Maggie's talking to her about real estate prices when your dad and Maggie's neighbor, Allen, brought her some fish. Seems like they had a good catch."

"I'm glad he got out and caught something. It seems the fishing around the lake has been off if you listen to the fishermen. I don't know why."

"We were talking about that, and Allison Wells said the Corps has been dumping chemicals around the dam to get rid of the zebra mussels. It has either killed off the fish or they've headed to clearer waters. Anyway, I didn't call to talk to a pregnant lady about chemicals. How about lunch soon? What are you doing Saturday?"

"Ouch!" Bernadette yelped into the phone. "Sorry, I just pinned myself, but no blood on the fabric. Saturday should be good. I'll be at Mom and Dad's. Pick me up?"

"Sure, let's plan on it. Talk to you later," Erin said into the phone and then clicked off.

The next call she needed to make was to Sheriff Montgomery.

She dialed, and he picked up immediately.

"Hey, Erin, how are you today?" Montgomery's booming voice came through her phone.

"I'm good, Sheriff, and you"

"Not bad. What can I do for you?"

Erin paused to collect her thoughts. "I was just visiting with Maggie, and Allison Wells was there. We were talking about the lake even though I was there to talk real estate prices. And they said the Corps of Engineers was dumping copper-based algaecides into the water near the dam. Is that the same chemical that was found in Jeff Larson's commuter cup?"

"Yeah, it was. Makes you think, huh? Who has access to that algaecide besides the Corps? So, I looked into it, and you can buy that in weaker form at any hardware store with the pool chemicals. Now what the Corps is using is probably stronger. But it isn't that hard to come by."

"Hum. I just met two employees of the Corps here at the lake. Rogers, whose voice is on the tape that Maggie had, and also Decker, the night shift guy. He was a trip. Rude. Slammed the door in my face and seemed skittish."

The Sheriff chuckled. "You thinking of changing professions? I mean if you want to get into law enforcement, I could always use another hand. I'd hire you in a heartbeat."

"Thanks, Sheriff. But I think I'll stick to law on the courthouse side. I couldn't hit the broadside of a barn with a gun. I'd probably shoot myself in the foot. But when Allison said what she did about copper-based algaecides, I had to ask. It's not like you hear about that chemical every day. I don't know about Rogers. He might be a standup guy—or maybe not. But that Decker character is flakey. That is just intuition and doesn't mean a thing, but he freaked me out."

"Intuition is half this job around here. I'll see what I can find out about Mr. Decker."

"Thanks, Sheriff. I'll keep digging," Erin said and clicked off.

Chapter 33

Bob Decker took out the trash from his rented bungalow. Most of it belonged to his roommate who never cleaned up after himself. He left dirty dishes in the sink and wet clothes in the washer. Basically, he was a slob. But Decker needed him—at the moment.

When Decker first moved to Keystone, he lived in a cheap mobile home that was cold in the winter and hot in the summer. There was little insulation from the winter winds, and the air conditioner barely kept up in the heat and humidity of eastern Oklahoma. But the rent for the trailer was cheap, until the landlord decided to sell. Decker couldn't afford to buy. So, he had to look in town for a place to rent and someone to help with the bills.

He found a roommate in the online classifieds. He didn't want to share the two-bedroom house, but the roommate worked days and he worked nights. Basically, they never saw each other. But there was plenty of debris in the wake of the man he shared the house with. Many times, Decker tossed his roommate's soured, wet clothes that had been in the washer for days into the dryer. Then he dumped the man's clothes on his unmade bed.

He wrote a note and threw it on the bed with the laundry. "I need the washer and dryer too. Don't leave your stuff in the washer. If it stinks, that's your fault." He knew he'd never see the roommate when the note was read.

Now the man wanted to bring a cat into the house. That would mean litter boxes to clean and torn and ragged furniture, drapes, and furballs on the floor. And he knew who would do the cleaning. He really didn't like cats. But at least they took care of themselves better than a dog. You had to train a dog and let it out. You couldn't train a cat. Yeah, when he got the promotion Shipley had promised, the roommate had to go. Decker's name was the only one on the lease.

Dishes drying in the drainer, his clothes in the washer, he pulled out the vacuum and ran it over the living room and his bedroom. Then he'd tackle the bathroom. They only had one, and it always had toothpaste in the sink and a ring around the tub. He should charge the roommate a cleaning fee. But he wouldn't. He wasn't used to ordering people around, and it wouldn't work anyway. They communicated with notes left on the bed or kitchen counter.

Rent had become impossible to pay on a single salary, and then there was Mom. Her Social Security check barely paid for the lousy nursing home where she lived, and he sometimes had to help her out. Trips to the beauty shop and some medications often went unpaid if he didn't step in. At least she had a bed and food. That was about all. But soon he'd make more money and he'd be able to take better care of Mom—and maybe throw out his roommate. He didn't want much in life—but a decent living.

He'd met Shipley late one night when the man banged on the door of the dam. No one ever did that. But Shipley introduced himself and said he had been watching how hard Decker worked. How he always showed up on time and took care of things. His boss at the Corps never said that. And Shipley said he needed a man like that to help with the empire he was building. From the sound of it, the empire was to be sprawling. Decker said yes—of course he wanted in on the ground floor of the venture. He could see the resort in his future.

He'd never been a violent man. He'd never had to be. But the bait and tackle guy wouldn't sell, and that ruined his chances of moving up. He was an old man, and his days were numbered anyway. Then there was his fishing buddy. He just added a little algaecide to the man's cup that he knew he'd eventually drink. But Decker wasn't there when he died so he couldn't be held responsible, right? Anyway, Shipley was supposed to go fishing with him that night—not him. No one knew he was on the dock before the Beck guy went out alone. Still, he felt guilty. He could have said no when his boss told him to get rid of them. But that wasn't in his nature either. He was used to doing what he was told.

His mom had told him he'd never amount to anything without a college education. But college was expensive, and he couldn't afford it. Shipley didn't ask him for credentials. Shipley just said he was a good worker, and they were hard to find. Decker didn't get many compliments. He grabbed on with both hands to the ones he did get. And this one was a doozy. He was moving up, and it was about time.

The new hotel was coming with or without him and maybe a new dam. He'd have to learn the new job, but he could do that. Mr. Shipley said he'd be a part of it. Maybe he'd be in charge of security or something else at the hotel. He dreamed of moving up from night shift at the dam to something else. Something in the sunshine!

He'd ask the boss next time what he had in mind for a man who had worked as hard as he had for the guy who owned all the best lakeside real estate on the lake. Yes, it was time to ask what his duties would include—and then ask for a raise. He'd earned it.

Chapter 34

Chris pulled down to the marina parking lot and looked around. Slips could be rented to keep your boat in if you didn't have a dock at home like his parents. He stepped out of the car and walked down the dock to the moorings and looked around. The marina not only housed boats, some with covered parking, others not, they did maintenance and storage. And if they were lucky, they also sold a boat or two. The bigger boats were on the other side, and he walked that way. What would he say if a salesman approached him? Was he looking to buy a boat? No, he wanted to know if his brother-in-law had or was about to. Not that it was any of his business, but lately he'd began to wonder about the man who married his sister. According to Uncle Jeff's notes, Ted was to meet him at the dam the night he died. But he didn't go out fishing with Uncle Jeff that night. What happened?

Chris was surprised that the bank had allowed Ted to borrow more money than he might be able to repay. He was buying up land that was underwater. Did the bank know it was underwater? That could be considered a shrewd business deal, unless you knew the people he was cheating. And now he was trying to buy a yacht. Ted didn't have money for a yacht, and Chris couldn't imagine what he would do with it if he bought it.

The water lapped at the edge of the dock where the

boats sat tethered to their slips. Huge vessels rocked in the water with names on the back of them. His family never got around to naming their boat. Hope had mentioned naming it *The African Queen*, but Dad said that boat sank so it was bad luck. Chris said they should name it *The Black Pearl*, but their boat was red—or crimson and cream. After all it was an Oklahoma boat. So, the boat remained unnamed like most of the boats on the lake. Most people only named yachts.

He'd always heard myths about it being bad luck not to name a boat. Most people ignored those ideas these days. He couldn't remember the last time he saw a family with a picnic lunch pull up to the island in a fish and ski rig with a name on it. But he heard it was bad luck to sail on a boat without a name. It was also bad luck to rename a boat (unless the proper name purging and renaming ceremonies were performed). It was bad luck to name a boat something brash or arrogant. You should stay away from names that would tempt the sea. Boat names like Victory, Millionaire, or Hurricane might tempt Poseidon himself. People and myths. They always said they didn't believe them, but still, the bigger the boat, the more likely it would get named. Maybe before he left he should name his parents' boat—just to be safe. It was time.

The big vessel on the end said *All In* on the back. *All In* like you bet your last dollar on it? Maybe a little brash. He smiled to himself thinking anyone who could afford a boat like that probably wasn't spending their last dollar.

He stared at the boat in the midday sun when a man in tan shorts and a dirty tee shirt stepped off. Probably the hired help. He pulled off his sunglasses and wiped the sweat from his brow and looked up.

Chris suddenly realized he was staring at his brother-in-law, Ted.

Startled, he almost stepped behind a post and then wondered why. He could talk to Ted—after all they were family.

"Ted?" Chris called out.

The man jerked his head around at his name and paused, then smiled. "Hi, Chris. What brings you down to the dock? Looking to buy a boat?"

"Oh, just looking at how the other half lives, I guess. Nice one there." Chris nodded to the vessel Ted had just come from.

"Yes it is. A buddy of mine is selling it. It would be nice, huh?"

"Yes, it would. *All In*, huh? It even sounds impressive." Chris eyed the man who'd been a member of his family for years, and somehow he got a chill in the afternoon sun.

"I guess." He paused. "Gotta go. I have a client waiting." Ted brushed past in a hurry and trotted up the dock toward the parking lot. "Good to see you," he called over his shoulder.

Some things about Ted just didn't add up. Chris had known him for years, but maybe he only thought he knew him.

Chapter 35

There was only one realtor in the town of Mannford, and Erin was sure that was where Ted hung his hat. Up on the hill near the grocery store sat the small and unassuming office in the strip mall beside the childcare center. She'd go by and ask if he was in. She wondered if his boss knew he was setting up a company that would be in competition with the one where he worked. But he had the right to go out on his own if he wanted to.

Opening the glass door, she found a cluttered office with the secretary on the phone. The woman continued to talk but raised her eyebrows at Erin in question as if she were asking what she wanted.

"Ted Shipley?" Erin spoke quietly and hoped the woman heard her.

The secretary nodded to the one office with the door open and Erin walked that way.

Inside sat the man she saw at the restaurant the night she met Ryan. He ran a hand through his blond hair as he shuffled through paperwork stacked high on his desk.

"Mr. Shipley?" Erin spoke, and he looked up. An instant smile plastered on his face.

"Yes, I'm Ted Shipley. What can I do for you?"

She wondered if he remembered her from the town meeting but introduced herself anyway. "I'm Erin Sampson, an attorney from Tulsa. I grew up in Mannford."

He looked confused. “Yes, I think you were at the townhall meeting recently. What can I do for you?”

“I wondered, since you’re a real estate agent, do you know who T & H Realty, LLC is? I’ve seen the business card. And we’ve found that name on a lot of deeds of land that have sold lately.”

He sat up straight and then slowly leaned back in his chair, eyeing her with impossibly blue eyes. He tapped a pencil on the desk. “You want to know who T & H Realty is, huh? You’re a lawyer. You can find that out yourself, why ask me?”

“Since you’re in the business, I just thought you might know the competition.”

Silence hung like a shroud.

Erin shuffled her feet, made herself stop, and then spoke again. “You’re right. I can find that out on my own. And I contacted the Secretary of State and found out that T & H Realty is owned by you and your wife, Hope. The address of the company is your home address.”

His face flashed guilt, then he resumed his calm manner. “So, what if I do own a realty company? There’s nothing illegal about that.” He got up and walked around the desk to where she stood by the door.

Erin moved away from the door and looked at the chair in front of the desk that he had not offered her. He didn’t want her to stay.

Shipley stood facing her with his hand on the doorknob and stared at her. “Like I said, T & H Realty and what it buys is not illegal and should be of no concern to an attorney from Tulsa. This is Mannford, not the big city. So, what is it that you want?” His demeanor had changed to one of confrontation—the smile long gone.

"I represent the Sunset Hills Homeowners' Association, and they are concerned about the sale of property around the lake. With all the flooding it seemed that many properties were changing hands."

"And…"

"And they were all bought by T & H Realty for rock bottom prices. That is what concerns the homeowners' association and the bank. The bank owns the mortgages to many of the properties. The value of property around this lake has dropped dramatically, and you can imagine how that must make current owners and the bank feel. They are afraid that the value of their property will drop even more because of the sale of land around them. The price of current land sales obviously affects the price of future sales."

Shipley's blue eyes became darker, and his face reddened. "You and the bank think you have it all figured it out. Did it occur to you that maybe T & H Realty did their neighbors a favor by buying up their flooded land that they couldn't use anymore? Because that is what happened. T & H Realty was approached, and land was sold. It was as simple as that. And there is nothing you or the bank can do about it. It was all legal and above board."

"So, you plan to sell the property back to the owners once the flooding is over? At an increase in price?"

His face became even darker. "What T & H Realty does with the property that is owned is of no concern to you, the homeowners' association, or the bank. It was bought fair and square." He gestured toward the door. "Now if you will excuse me, I have work to do." He nodded for her to leave.

He was right. He could buy the property for less than appraised value as long as the bank would loan him money. But the bank had cut him off. He wouldn't be able to buy any more unless he could convince another bank to make him a loan. She just wished she knew his plans.

"Okay, for now. I'll be back in touch if I have any other questions." Erin left, feeling his eyes shooting darts into her as she walked away. He was guilty of something, she was sure. But of what?

Chapter 36

Friday afternoon

There it stood. The last piece of property Ted needed to buy before finalizing his plans for the hotel. No, not just a hotel, a resort—the biggest in the state. The one last piece of the pie. The plot of land near the current grocery store that nobody wanted sat empty except for an ancient trailer with the tongue still sticking out the front. Most self-respecting homeowners would have taken the tongue off and stored it underneath the trailer for when the home was moved again. But this one had sat there so long a sapling had grown up inside the fork. Now the sapling was a mature tree pressing itself into the metal and growing around it on one side. The other side of the tree squashed the dilapidated trailer caving it in and allowing rain and vegetation to invade. It was a mess and needed to just be hauled off—after the tree was cut down. The owner obviously didn't want it, they just didn't want to sell. Typical.

There was a storm in the forecast for tonight, and it was the perfect time to finish off this piece of property. If anyone investigated a fire, it would appear it came from lightning—that is if they bothered after the flooding. And with the lake already full to the brim it wouldn't be long before the dam had to be rebuilt. His days of groveling for pennies were almost over. And the attorney who visited today was getting too close. It was time to end this mess and get on down the road.

The breeze was light, but inside the maze of vegetation, it was hardly felt at all. They had a chance of precipitation again tonight so he wanted to get this done early before the rain could put it out. He brushed away the spiderweb that wrapped itself around his hat. A pile of wood and leaves lay in the middle of the lot near the decaying trailer. It was just the place for a match.

He'd parked his car at the store and hiked the quarter mile path into the deserted lot. He didn't see anyone he knew, but it was a small town, and you just never knew who might be watching. So, he waited.

The bugs were relentless. Starving mosquitos and biting flies swarmed his face—he batted them away and pulled the insect repellant from his back pocket lathering up his head and neck. It seemed to slow them down for a while, but the perspiration that rolled down his face and stung his eyes soon called them back into action. He couldn't take much more of this. He needed to get this done and be on his way.

The small bottle of lighter fluid he brought with him should be enough to get the kindling started. He only wanted a small fire. Just enough to get rid of the broken trailer. Finding a stick, he stirred the leaves to see what lay beneath. The wood was rotted and some of it was moist, but there should be just enough dry leaves—along with the lighter fluid—to start a small, smoldering fire.

Glancing behind him one more time he knew he was alone. He leaned over and squirted the liquid onto the pile. The acrid smell burned his nose and his already stinging eyes. He flung the empty can into the water and struck the match from the small matchbook he'd shoved in his pocket earlier. It would take a while, but if he were lucky, the fire would clear the old trailer and the empty lot. Maybe then the owners would sell. After all, what good was the lot after the trailer and all the vegetation was gone? Who would want a burned-out hull that would have to be hauled away? He would, but it was best not to show his hand to a potential buyer.

Slowly the flames began to rise from the pile of leaves, mostly burning off the lighter fluid, but soon it began to catch on the wood and leaves around it. Ted smiled and backed away. He'd leave now and let nature take its course. When he stepped out of the dense vegetation, his body immediately cooled, and he wiped his face with the bandana he'd tied around his neck.

He could get home and slip in the back way for a quick shower in time to show his lovely bride the surprise he had for her—the boat he'd just purchased. It was a great price, and there was no time like the present to take it for a spin. The name was *All In.* That was the final straw when he saw the name, he knew he had to have it. *All In* was not only the name of the boat, but it was also a good name for the life he was building. He was all in on this one. It had to work.

Yes, he knew his timing was right.

It was their anniversary. Surely, Hope wouldn't argue with him tonight.

Reaching the car, he climbed in smelling like sweat and insect repellant. He rolled down his window. Reaching in the glove box, he pulled the bottle out and unscrewed the lid. He took a long swig in celebration. He'd just set in motion the sale of the last piece of land he needed. He replaced the lid and shoved the bottle back in the glove box then drove off down the road toward home.

He never noticed the wind shift that began to blow the other way sucking the flames with it.

Chapter 37

Sweat ran down Erin's back as she pedaled. Going by the gym after work was a good idea especially when Rob was working late. She didn't want to stay at work, even though she could always find something to do. She didn't want to just curl up and watch a movie alone at their apartment. Rob wasn't home, Aunt Toni had a date, and Mom was out with Brent. She would be alone. But Erin didn't like just sitting alone and waiting for Rob, so she went to the gym she'd joined of late. Recently she'd noticed her work pants were getting snug, and she had a wedding coming up. Wiping the sweat from her eyes, she increased her speed.

"Hey, lady. I think you have the good bike tonight. I hated the one I ended up on last time. The seat was too narrow." Ryan climbed on the bike next to her.

"Hi, Ryan. I didn't know you came here."

Ryan adjusted the seat to the correct height. "Sometimes. Not as much as I should. You know, I just overheard someone in the locker room talking about Shipley. You might know her. I think she works in the Register of Deeds office in the courthouse. I'm sure that's where I've seen her before. Anyway, she said 'Ted Shipley owns most of Keystone Lake these days.' I thought we were the only ones who knew that. But she does file the deeds for the county."

Erin nodded. "We saw all the property deeds from

around the lake, and most of them said T & H Reality. I talked to him recently, and he acted guilty as hell. I just don't know of what." Erin found herself slowing down as she talked to Ryan. She sat back on the bike and let the wheel spin as she rested. "Maybe we need to check into him more. I know it's not illegal to own property around a lake, but just look at all the people who have left—and he just happens to own their land now. I'm sure the bank where he gets his money won't talk without a subpoena, and we have no reason for one. But something just feels off to me."

Ryan began to pedal. "He works for a realtor, right? I mean he shows property to other people and helps them buy it. That's what most realtors do. That is how they make their money. They get a percentage of the price of the property when it sells. But as far as I knew, the people who left didn't have their property up for sale. I mean I don't run around looking at for sale signs, but from listening to the people talk, property owners just up and left when the water got too high. Who does he work for anyway?"

Erin shrugged. "I don't know the name of the realtor, the only one in Mannford. Mom just always called it the real estate office because there was only one. We can Google it. I'd ask Mom but she and Brent are always running off to do something when they aren't working."

"It's good she has someone, though, right?" asked Ryan.

"Of course. She was alone long enough. Speaking of enough, I think I've had enough of this thing," Erin said gesturing to the bike. "You want it? I'm hitting the showers."

Ryan slowed her bike and climbed off as Erin prepared to walk away. “Let me know if you hear anything, okay?”

“Will do,” Erin said and walked away. She’d talk to Mom and see how many of those lake properties had a for sale sign or if someone just sold them to Shipley. He said they were offered. Maybe the sale had been his suggestion. Maybe they really didn’t plan on selling until he mentioned it. He worked for a realtor and was privy to people wanting to sell their property. There was nothing illegal about that. There was nothing illegal about one person snatching up properties that were underwater these days, either. After all, who would want them. Unless it was someone who knew how the normal lake levels looked. Someone who had been around a long time. Something just wasn’t right, but she had no idea what.

Glancing out the plate glass window she noticed the wind blowing the trees across the street and how dark the sky was getting. More rain was coming, and the area didn’t need that.

Chapter 38

Hope would drop off the kids with Mom and Dad to spend the night. It was their anniversary, and she and Ted needed some time away. She did, anyway. It seemed Ted was becoming more and more distant, and his drinking sometimes increased when he worked late. She wondered if he was really working—like he said—but she knew it was often important to socialize with the client in order to seal the deal in real estate. She had considered getting her real estate license at one time. But that was three kids ago. She loved her kids and never wanted anyone to feel she gave up anything for them. But there was the nagging feeling that she never talked to anyone over the age of six anymore. That might have been an exaggeration. She talked to people at church and the grocery store—not to mention her mother—but a little social time would be nice.

It was amazing they had been married seven years. It was a whirlwind romance, and she was thrilled when he popped the question. Her mother asked if she was sure. He wasn't from around here, like most of the little town people, and maybe that was what she liked about him. He was new and interesting. Seven years. And most of them were good. The children were wonderful.

She had no idea what Ted had planned for their anniversary, but she put on a nice sundress and sandals. Not too dressy, but nice enough for a restaurant in Tulsa.

She hoped he was taking her out to eat.

When they married seven years ago, she worked as a receptionist for a doctor in town. It was an easy job and brought in a little money. She knew she could do that and more. She never intended to have her children so quickly—or so many. And now she'd have to bring in a fortune just to pay for daycare. She knew she needed to work. They needed the money. She'd even thought about putting in a home daycare and taking in a couple more kids, but that required a license these days and insurance, supplies, food, all things that cost money she didn't have. Even if she hired an au pair, and she didn't have a place for them to live with the family, she'd have to make enough to pay the person and still come out ahead. There were a couple of day care places in town. She wondered what kind of certificate she'd need to babysit for someone else's kids, and could she bring her own to work? Would her own children warm up to that kind of situation, or would they be jealous of her time with other children? No, for now she was a stay-at-home mom. Maybe someday when the kids were old enough to take care of themselves, or just attend school all day, she could go back to work. Her biggest goal these days was not to have any more children. Five was more than enough and whether she worked or not, she and Ted had to take care of the ones they had. She needed to bring up the idea again with Ted about permanent birth control. She could have the surgery. She knew Mom would help out for a little while afterward. Maybe she'd do it in the summer when Mom wasn't in class. Or Ted could get a vasectomy. Of course, she knew he wouldn't. This would be up to her.

But tonight, wasn't the time to bring it up. They

argued too much these days about bills and things. It was an anniversary for heaven's sake. Seven years. People talked about the seven-year itch. She knew she didn't have an itch for someone else. Ted was enough. Sometimes he was a handful, but she didn't want to start over with someone new. They were a couple, a family, and a family was all she'd ever wanted.

She glanced once more in the mirror and then walked to the living room where the television kept the children occupied while she prepared for the evening. They were going to their grandparents for the night. Thank God for grandparents or she'd never be able to get away. She felt a small pang of guilt over wanting to get away from her own children. But she should have a life too sometimes, right?

"Okay, everyone have what they want to take to grandma's? Remember you only get to take one thing."

Her beautiful children sat on the floor next to the baby's swing watching cartoons. Baby Sarah watched the cartoons as intently as her older siblings.

"Hello. Anyone listening?"

"Cartoons!" Emory said excitedly.

"Yes, I'm sure Grandma has cartoons too and some of your movies. You can watch at her house. Let's get in the car. Grab the toy you're taking to Grandma's, and we'll get out of here."

She'd already taken their overnight bags to the car. Clicking off the T.V., she herded the kids to the minivan for a night at Grandma's.

"Thanks for taking care of the munchkins tonight, Mom." Hope hugged her mom as her dad found the right movie for the kids to watch. He knew what they liked, and he'd play it no matter how many times he'd seen it before.

Back in the minivan she drove home the long way on the road along the lake. She knew Ted would be late. He always was these days. She saw the yachts moored at the dock. She couldn't imagine how much money one of them cost.

"I'm home," she called as she came in the door. She'd seen Ted's car in the drive. When he didn't answer, she called again and walked up the stairs to the bedroom. He was just coming from the shower in his pants with a towel draped over his head. He still looked as good shirtless as he had the first time she'd seen him. She smiled and walked to him. He was still moist from the shower.

"Happy anniversary," she said as she wrapped her arms around him and smelled the alcohol on his breath over the toothpaste he'd just used. It was going to be one of those nights. But she'd try to be nice.

Chapter 39

"I know there's rain on the way, but with the kids here, I need to go to the grocery store. We at least need some milk and bread." Maggie picked up her purse digging for the car keys.

The kids sat on the floor eyes glued to a movie they'd seen hundreds of times at Grandma's. They always insisted on watching the same one.

Chris stood putting down the daily paper. It had been years since he'd sat in a recliner and read the paper. He might get used to this if he wasn't careful. He needed a little something to do. "It might be faster to take the boat to the convenience store than to drive to the store in town. It's gassed up and ready to go." Since he arrived, he'd spent many hours going through the boat and making minor repairs, preserving the wood accents and polishing the brass. It looked like a new vessel.

"That would be great. Do you mind?" Maggie stood in the doorway wearing shorts and flip flops after changing from work clothes. "Paul, you'll stay with the kids until we get back?"

Paul pulled his head from the fridge and came out with a bottle of water. "Sure, I'll be here. We'll grill some burgers for dinner. Get some cheese while you're there. I noticed it's almost gone, and you can't have cheeseburgers without cheese."

The afternoon sun sparkled on the water as the boat

skimmed across the lake. Chris glanced at his mom. She sat smiling. He wondered how often she boated on the lake she loved. He knew she swam in the cove, but with Dad gone all the time, Mom probably didn't take the boat out by herself. With Uncle Jeff gone now, and all the hours Dad was gone, Chris knew his mom would be alone more than normal. Thankfully, she was still working. Her job was important to her.

Quickly they pulled up at the side of the convenience store where he ran into Ryan a few days earlier. He smiled again thinking of her standing on the dock with the sun shining through red-gold hair.

Jumping onto the deck from the front of the boat, he tied it up then helped his mom step out.

"I'll be right back," she said, walking toward the store.

Chris leaned against a pier staring out at the beautiful lake. It was like glass, and the light sparkled off the surface as if it were covered in diamonds. To the west, thunderclouds built. The calm before the storm, he thought and hoped his mom hurried with her shopping.

Glancing toward the store he realized he couldn't see his mom inside. She said she'd be right back. Maybe she needed help carrying what she bought. Shoppers came and went. Most with beer or a picnic essential. Mom probably ran into some one she knew.

Opening the door, he heard his mother's voice.

"Oh, I'd love to see your roses, Sally. Maybe next week sometime after the grandkids go home. I could come by after work someday."

His mom stood at the counter with three bags of groceries ready to carry out. The woman she'd been speaking to was leaving as he came in.

Chris reached for the bags. “Ready? It looks like that weather is coming in faster than we thought.”

“Sure. Oh, do you mind if we go home the long way? I want to see if I can spot Sally’s roses. They are over near the dam. I don’t know if you remember where her place is.”

“If we hurry. I don’t want to get caught in the rain.” They walked back to the boat, and his mom stepped in then turned to take the groceries from his hands. He handed one bag to her and then climbed in. Once she had the sacks stowed, he untied the boat from its moorings.

Chris climbed into the seat, started the engine, and backed out slowly. He spun the boat in the direction of the dam. The sky darkened behind them.

“Sally says the rose bush we gave her when her husband died is right out front near the dock and in full bloom. It is a brilliant yellow. I hoped to see it before the storm takes its toll.”

Chris raced across the lake thankful for the calm water. Slowing, he rounded the corner of the cove. There, next to the dock, the sun shone down on the roses at Sally’s dock glowing a lemon yellow.

“Oh, they’re beautiful! Just look at how big the bush has gotten!”

Chris glanced at his mom, once more slowing the boat. He didn’t want to leave a wake rushing in the cove where people lived and swam. And his mom was right. The bush was in full bloom. The way the sun shone through the petals made him wish he had his camera.

“I’d like to put a bush down by our dock. I wonder if it would grow in that area.”

Chris nosed the boat into the cove and began a slow turn. “I don’t know why not. Your roses grow about any place you put them." Then his eyes were drawn to the sky. "Uh oh, we better get moving or we're going to get wet." He pointed to the west, and his mom held her hand up to shade her eyes.

"Oh, my. That is moving fast. Yes, we'd better hurry. I don't know if we'll cook hamburgers out tonight or not."

Moving slowly out of the cove, Chris pushed the throttle forward as soon as they were clear and into the body of the lake—when he saw the first signs of fire on the shore across the lake.

"Mom, look." He pointed out the flames.

Up on the hill on the other side of the lake, the forest was on fire. The wind increased, and flames licked along the shore toward the homes that dotted the landscape.

"Oh no! What started that? Do you think someone had a campfire? That entire section of houses could go up. I wonder if the fire department knows about it?"

Maggie pulled her phone from her pocket and began to dial. Chris could hear her talking when the wind shifted, and the sky darkened quickly. He glanced west and realized he had instinctively slowed the boat to see the fire. They both stared at the fire that spread quickly on the other side of the lake. Was that the grocery store in flames? Whatever it was, this weather was coming in fast, and he needed to get them to safety.

"We've got to get out of here. We can't do anything about the fire, but those clouds don't look friendly. Besides, a good hard rain will put out the fire." He once again pushed the throttle forward and raced across the lake when the first crack of lightning lit up the sky and thunder shook the boat. He pointed the boat toward home. They might get wet, but they'd try to stay ahead of the storm.

****

After leaving the gym, Ryan drove toward home using the back roads and thinking about the lake and what she and Erin had uncovered. She wanted to talk to Chris again about the purchase of the boat. Her contact at the bank said they weren't going to loan him money—but he might have gone somewhere else. Sometimes the yacht company did their own finance.

Ryan knew that Chris' parents were aware of their relationship again. At least she thought it was a relationship. She was unsure. But when she got to their house, she was uncertain about how to approach asking if Chris was home. If he didn't answer the door, she'd be facing his parents and that made her nervous, she thought as she pulled into the driveway. She stepped up on the deck. She heard the noise of the TV. It was silly to be embarrassed showing up again after all these years, but she was. It wasn't as if she'd visited his parents after the breakup, but she'd seen them around town. And now she was back. She knocked on the door hoping Chris would hear her car and come to the door himself.

But he didn't. The door opened, and Paul Beck stood there smiling.

"Come in, Ryan. Chris took his mom to the grocery store. I expect them back soon. It looks like rain." Paul opened the door wide.

Ryan stepped into the kitchen—the one she'd been in many times as a kid—and peeked around the corner. All five grandkids were on the floor watching the TV. They were mesmerized by the movie and didn't even look up. "I see you have the babysitting gig tonight."

Paul smiled. "Yeah, and happy to do it. You want to

come in and wait?"

Ryan paused. "No, I think I'll head home. Tell him I was by, okay?" She stepped back out of the door.

"Will do." Paul looked at the sky. "Better hustle, you might get wet."

She waved as she walked across the deck toward her car, happy Paul hadn't tried to ask questions about a renewed relationship she was unsure of.

As she climbed in the car, the rain began.

Chapter 40

Friday night

The higher-than-normal water levels hid the rocks, and Chris saw them too late. With the storm approaching it was almost dark, and he should have been off the water by now. He tried to swerve but miscalculated how far they jutted out of the dark water. But the rocks found the boat—and suddenly stopped it dead in the water. Chris flew into the steering wheel and knocked the air from his lungs. The half-crouched position—almost standing—he was in as he steered the boat helped him see over the water-splattered windshield. The same windshield that just crashed into his head. Thrown sideways, he didn't know how long he lay wedged into what used to be the boat and his mother's seat, but he slowly sat up. That's when he realized—his mother was not in the seat next to him. Where was she?

"Mom!" All he could hear was the wind. The broken boat was taking on water. Waves rocked it back and forth against the rocky shore. "Mom!" Holding his head, Chris slopped through ankle-deep and rising water toward what used to be the nose of the boat. The water threatened to suck off his wet deck shoes as he climbed out on to the rocky shore. Rocks were slimy in the warm summer evening. Climbing out of what was left of the boat and slipping on jagged points of granite, he called again. She was in the boat with him when he hit the rocks, she must have been thrown free. He had to find her quickly. It was getting darker.

Maybe he should go back and look through the boat again. Maybe she was in the back. And then he heard a gasp. He jerked his head around toward the noise out in the water.

"Chris! Where are you?" Maggie splashed the water around her.

"I'm here, Mom. Are you okay?" He called out into the water in the direction of her voice, still not able to see her. It seemed to take forever climbing over rocks and broken pieces of boat back into the dark water where his mother stood waist deep in the lake. She stumbled forward and crashed into him pushed from behind by a wave. She shivered, and he looked at her in the darkness of the weather. "I couldn't find you. Are you okay?"

"I think so. Just got the wind knocked out of me. You?" Her voice trembled.

"Yeah, I think so." He grabbed her, pulled her forward, and hugged her close. "I was so scared. I couldn't find you. I'm so sorry. I didn't see the rocks until it was too late." He felt like a little boy explaining an accident that broke her favorite vase.

"I didn't see them either. The water levels have fluctuated so much lately."

"Mom, about the boat…" Chris felt like a child explaining to his mother. He knew he had just destroyed his parents' boat. After all, he was driving when it hit the rocks and splintered.

"It doesn't matter, we're alive and it was insured. We'll worry about it later." She turned back and looked across the water. "That fire is getting worse."

He stood in thigh-deep water looking out into the dark lake. Chris wiped the blood from his eyes. Head wounds always bled worse than anything even if the wound was superficial. But he had to get Mom somewhere safe. It was dark, and the rocks were between them and the shore. Once up on the bank, he had to find a way home. If they took the road, it would be a much longer route home, but cross-country they could run into fences, ravines, anything.

"I don't know. Looks like the grocery store area. But we've got to find a way home. I think if we can get over those rocks and up on the bank, we should be able to get to the road. Maybe we'll run into a neighbor or someone to give us a ride." He grabbed her hand and pulled her to the rocks where the waves crashed. Slowly they found their way up and over pieces of sharp rocks that were dumped there to save the shore from erosion. Chris counted it a win that neither had a broken bone when they reached the top in the dark.

Once up on the bank the weather changed immediately. Wind whipped through the oak trees that never lost their leaves, even in winter, until new ones took their place. Waves beat the water into a frenzy. The cove they were stranded in without a boat became a fury of white water, tossing bits and pieces of broken fiberglass boat onto the rocks. It was a good thing they were out of the water.

An explosion on the other side of the lake threw a fireball into the air. The area was littered with propane tanks that fueled homes. The small fire burst into several huge ones racing away from the water and toward homes, gobbling all in its path.

"Oh, the Smiths!" Maggie stopped and gazed across

the lake at the red glow where her neighbors' home stood.

"I'm sure they aren't home. It's not the weekend yet. We've got to get to shelter before this storm really gets started." Chris grabbed his mother's hand once again as the lightning cracked open the sky. A transformer exploded in the distance illuminating the town at the end of Basin Road. Emergency sirens blew, and the tiny fire department rushed to overwhelming fires. Storm warning horns, barely heard over the wind, warned citizens to take cover, whether from the storm or the fire, it was hard to tell.

Climbing up the hill toward what should be the road, Chris stopped and helped his mother time and again. He had to remind himself she wasn't as young as him and didn't lead the rustic existence he sometimes did. Blood ran into Chris's shoes from the scrapes of thorn bushes. His head, where he hit when thrown forward, ached mercilessly but he kept going.

"Ah!" A voice behind him caused Chris to twist around—and his mother was gone.

"Mom!"

A groan. "I'm okay. Just stumbled." She stood up in the dark and took a step crying out in pain. "And maybe twisted my ankle."

Why couldn't he at least have a flashlight? He leaned over to look at his mother's ankle as lightning lit up the sky. It wasn't misshapen, and no bones protruded. "I doubt that it's broken. Lean on me, and we'll get out of this mess."

In typical Maggie fashion, she walked under her own power only leaning on Chris when necessary. The first step a hop, she soon began to put weight on the painful ankle. Chris knew his mother could endure pain. She never wanted to show weakness, and they trudged on.

They finally found the blacktop that led from the lake to the road, and walking was much easier. The incline was steep, but they continued uphill as fast as they could. The wind was at their backs blowing off the water. If the winds changed direction, the fire would follow. Thank God it was on the other side of the lake, and they weren't trying to outrun the fire and the storm.

Travel was slow, and Chris often grabbed Maggie's hand to help her up the hill. The old trailer that the family once owned years ago was at the top of the hill. It belonged to a weekend couple now, but Chris knew where they used to hide a key—if it was still there. He could smell rain in the distance and knew they would soon be soaked once more.

Chapter 41

The night was dark and almost moonless, except for a sliver that shown now and then through the clearing clouds. Hope had to admit the boat was gorgeous. *All In* it said on the back. But could they afford it? Ted always had bigger ideas than he had means to pay for them. She sat in the deck chair with a glass of wine in her hands. The sheer silvery wrap he'd given her as a gift wrapped around her bare shoulders. It was their anniversary, and she didn't want to upset him—he had worked so hard for this. The boat was practically a yacht with a sleeping berth and kitchen.

"So, what do you think? Don't you love her?" Ted leaned forward and looked at his wife with her long legs propped up on the ice chest and a glass of wine in her hand.

Hope sighed. "Ted, the bank called yesterday asking about last month's payment, and I said they would have to talk to you. I feel like it is my fault for not being more involved in the finances. I'm always busy with the kids. But if we can't make the payments we have now, how could we possibly take on more?" She knew he didn't like to be second guessed.

His face contorted before he sighed. "It's for you and the kids. I thought the family could use it for outings, and besides, when this new deal goes through there will be plenty of money. The bank can wait one more month.

The boat's a good price, so now is the time to buy." He drained the half-full wine glass and reached toward the ice chest.

Hope moved her feet to the deck and sat up. "Besides the fact that we don't have the money, I could never bring the kids out on this at their ages. Five kids are a handful on land, there's no way I would take them all out on a boat at one time. Someone would end up in the water." She watched him pour more wine in his glass—almost up to the rim, and then he offered to refill hers as well. She accepted. "I've got to say, though, it is a beautiful night and so luxurious lounging here with the waves rocking the boat. When do we have to have it back?"

"Tomorrow. But for tonight, no one knows where we are, and we're completely alone." He smiled showing pearly white teeth.

"So, what's going on that is going to pay out big soon?" Hope never asked questions about finances, but he had been extra secretive lately.

Ted looked out into the water taking another drag on his wine. "How would you feel about being the richest woman on the lake? Maybe the state?" He glanced at her out of the corner of his eye.

"Oh Ted. I'm already rich with you and our five kids. Money doesn't mean that much to me."

"You've always had it. When you haven't, it is a little bit more important."

Hope reached over to pat his hand, and he jerked away.

"Hope, just once, I wish you would believe in me. I'm buying up land in this area so I can put a resort on the peninsula where the rivers dump into the lake. It will be magnificent! It will bring in tourism like this area has never seen. We'll all be rich." He drained the glass again.

"Not everyone around here is going to like the tourism, and where are you going to get the money for a resort? Like I said, the bank called yesterday."

This was not how she wanted to spend her anniversary with the man she loved. The kids were at her mom's for the night while they were on this moonlight cruise. She hadn't even told Mom where she was going. She had her cell if she was needed.

"I'm sorry if the rednecks don't like progress, but they are just going to have to get used to it."

"Rednecks, really Ted? I mean they're our neighbors and, granted, some of them are a little less educated and a little poorer than the rest, but there is no need to belittle them."

"It's a good word for some of them. They might be able to educate their children if they tried a little harder to make a living. After this, there will be plenty of jobs for all of them." He huffed and looked at the empty wine glass, stood and went down into the hold of the boat. Hope could hear him in the galley rummaging through the fridge, and he came back out with another opened bottle of wine.

"You're going to feel awful in the morning if you keep drinking like that." Hope instantly closed her mouth when she looked at his face. It was clouded with rage like she had never seen before. This was, after all, their anniversary—and she was not being a very supportive wife.

"It's always something, isn't it, Hope? I mean why did you marry me when you don't believe in anything I say or do? Everything is wrong, even how I drink!

Between you and the attorney snooping around in my business today…" He turned the wine bottle up and drank from it, guzzling the liquid without benefit of a glass. Deep red liquid ran down the sides of his neck, and he wiped his face with the back of his hand. She had never seen him so agitated.

"I'm buying the boat, and you and the kids can stay home if you like. I'll take clients out in it. Clients who stay in the resort. The resort that makes us all rich." He was beginning to slur his words, his eyes glassy, he stared at his wife who sat dumfounded. A wave slopped up against the boat causing Ted to stumble grabbing the chair for support. Then he walked to the controls of the boat, started the engine, and began to bring up the anchor.

"Ted," Hope began as she stood and walked toward him. "Listen, I'm not trying to make you mad—especially on our anniversary. Let's just go try out the bed. You've had too much to drink, it is dark, and in the morning, this will all look much better. Come on, hon." She reached for his arm, and he pushed her away.

"No, this has been coming for some time. The kids and I'll be better off without you. You will never believe in me, and you don't understand what it is to be poor. I'll never be poor again, and I will crush anyone who gets in the way of my dreams!" His face dark even in the moonless night, he took hold of the hand that grasped his arm. He spun her and pushed her toward the back of the boat.

"Ted! You're hurting me, stop that!" She tried to pull away, but he jerked her back around facing him—then slapped her across the face. The sheer wrap fell from her shoulders. She saw stars flash before her eyes, then the dark night became darker before she could focus again, and her body sank toward the floor. Suddenly she was in the air—was she passing out from the blow?

And she hit the cool water feeling it close over her. Bubbles went up her nose, and she realized she was sinking. She was a good swimmer, but it took her by surprise—and then she heard the roar of the engine near her head. Instinctively she stroked away from the boat's engine and propeller that was much too close for comfort before realizing the boat was moving away from her. The yacht left her rocking in its wake—waves splashing over her face strangling her—as it sped away and toward the other side of the lake.

"Ted!" She called out over and over, but no one heard her over the roar of the boat. Swimming as fast as her arms and legs would carry her, her first thought was to try to catch up with the boat as it sped away in the dark. She knew it was stupid and, even if she were able to swim fast enough to catch the boat, Ted would not let her on. The push was no accident. Yes, he was drunk, but still, her husband threw her off the boat and drove away.

He left her—in the middle of a dark lake at night. He left his wife and the mother of his children to drown. He didn't mean to throw her overboard, did he? It was the wine. But even in shock, she knew better. He had left her for dead. Tears ran down her face mingling with the lake she'd known all her life.

She continued to tread water spinning around with blurry vision to see what was close that she could swim to, but all she could see was dark water and an equally black sky. Clouds would move and expose an occasional star, but there was nothing else. Her face stung where he hit her, and a dull ache was beginning on that side of her head. She realized she was panting and laid her head back looking at the sky. Breathing in, her lungs lifted her body as she tried to relax. The cool water made her face feel better where she had been struck—and then it hit her. Was she going to drown in the lake she grew up on?

She was a floater. Not the kind like police call a dead body found in the lake, but someone who floated easily in the water without much movement. Her mom told her that when she learned to swim—a floater like her mom. Chris sank to the bottom like a stone and always beat her when they dove to the bottom of the cove where they played. But he couldn't float on his back the way she could. As a kid she would float along on her back without an air mattress unless she was swamped by a large wave. Her brother used to swim underneath her and pull her down for spite. How she wished he were here with her now. He'd know what to do. She continued to lie on her back and stare up at the sky, getting colder by the minute. The wine she drank made her feel warm at first but probably thinned the blood bringing on hypothermia sooner. The evening had started out warm, but the clouds blew in and a fine mist began, chilling her to the bone.

Teeth rattling, she remembered an article she'd read. The military trained their swimmers in open water to curl into a ball to concentrate body heat to the core. But that was with the benefit of a life jacket. She had none and rolling into a ball did not help her float with her head above water. How long until daylight, and how long until a boater or lake patrol might find her? As it was, if a night-fisherman were out, he might run over her before he could see her in the water. She was better off alone until daylight.

She lifted her head, thinking she heard lapping. If

the water was lapping on the shore, she should swim in that direction. The wind picked up again chilling her more—if that was possible. She pulled her knees up and slowly began to sink. Once again she laid her head back listening—trying to decide which way to swim to the sound. And her head banged against something hard.

Gasping, her first thought was Ted had come back for her. Reaching behind her she brushed the rough, yet slimy, piece of driftwood log that might just be her rescuer. She clung to it knowing it was floating before it ran into her and chances were, it would continue to float. As a kid, she and Chris had often sat on logs that floated up in their cove. Once there was a snake on the log, and they both made a beeline to the shore. She tried not to think of the snake. There was no snake on this log, she told herself.

Using her arms, she pulled the log to her and laid the uninjured side of her head against the spongy bark, breathing a sigh of relief. She was no longer totally responsible for her floating, the log would hold her up. If the evening had been warm, she would have climbed on top, but instead she clung to it with her arms, letting her legs trail.

How long she lay like that she didn't know. She clung to the log dozing until she'd relaxed enough to almost let go, jerking her back to consciousness.

Chapter 42

Shipley navigated the dark water watching for land he knew in the daytime. It appeared different at night. Treacherous.

He thought briefly of Hope, who he left treading water, and contemplated going back. But by now, she'd be dead. She shouldn't have gotten in his way. Now he was certain his dream would come true. The one thing left in his way was gone. He'd say she fell overboard, they'd been drinking, and he looked for her for some time. Once he was certain she was gone, he headed home to seek help.

Shaking his head, he pulled himself back to the task at hand. The dam. He'd start to let the water out more quickly now. Once the water levels fell, the land would return, and only prime real estate would be left behind.

The rain came down harder as he negotiated the lake. Luckily, the dock wasn't that far away. He rounded the tip of land that jutted out, and his vision cleared enough to see the dock—lights still on. Constantly wiping the water from his eyes, he navigated the flooded cove. Old folks would call this a gully washer, toad strangler, flooding of epic proportions. Some parts of the dock were inaccessible. But there was a slip near the outside of the cove for this beauty, and it was about the only thing left that she could fit into. So many of the slips were flooded. But that would end soon.

It took two tries, but he pulled into the slip and quickly tied up the yacht, then ran for his car. He was already soaked, so he wondered why he ran. But there was a feeling of urgency. He'd get to the dam, open up the gates to full capacity and—just for safekeeping—take the blueprints home with him. There would be no one to snoop in his business now. The kids could be trusted. And they wouldn't know what it was anyway.

The kids. What would he tell the kids about their mother? But first he had to get the blueprints out of the dam and home with him.

****

Back on the road, Ryan passed by the boat dock where the big boats were kept. The slips were rented month to month, and some of them held yachts. Without thinking she slowed down and looked at the boats tied up and gently rocking in the waves. Someday, she'd like to own a sailboat. A small one. She'd learn to sail and spend her weekends on the water instead of sitting at a desk in an office without even a window. She was beginning to regret her career choice. The pay was good, but the hours at a desk could be grueling.

Ryan drove to the bottom of the hill and parked, looking longingly at the sail boats tied up when the light rain increased and began to pour. A boat was gliding into the cove and headed for a slip. *All In* it had painted on the back. That could be her someday, only a smaller version. It took two tries, but the obviously inexperienced pilot finally got the boat into position to slide into its place among the others.

She switched on the windshield wipers and watched as the man quickly tied up the vessel and then ran for his car in the rain. He was going to get wet. No, he was already wet.

The car was yellow and compact—not the kind of car a man with a yacht would drive. And then he looked up the hill. She recognized him. It was Ted Shipley. A real estate salesman could afford a yacht? Real estate salesmen who drove compact cars? There was something wrong about this guy. He pulled out of the parking place and flew past her up the hill. She wondered where he was headed in such a hurry. She backed up so she could follow him and see. Maybe he was late to dinner. But something seemed off.

Following the curvy roads up and down hills, she realized he was headed for the dam. She wanted to share this with Erin. Something seemed strange about his behavior—more strange than normal. Pushing the button, she dialed Erin's cell phone. Hands-free phones were great.

"Hello?" Erin said, sounding distracted.

"Erin, this is Ryan. I hope I'm not bothering you."

"Rob was working late, and I came by Mom's. No one is home, so I was about to head back to Tulsa. What's up?"

"I thought you'd like to know; I'm following Shipley, and he's headed to the dam. I have no idea what for, but it is after hours, and we have weather coming in. I stopped by Beck's to see Chris. He wasn't home, but as I left I came past the public dock. Shipley was bringing in a huge yacht and then after tying up he jumped in his car and headed for the dam. I don't know, it seemed odd that he could afford a yacht with all that land he's been buying. It was also strange he was going to the dam after hours instead of the direction of his home. I'm following him. Maybe he's meeting with the night shift guy who works there. Want to come?"

There was silence on the other end. "I'll meet you in the parking lot of Pier 51 and we'll see what he's up to. A yacht, huh? I didn't think the bank would loan him that kind of money. But maybe he has somewhere else to borrow. There's more than one lending establishment."

"Yes there is, and I don't know what we'll be able to find out, but it seemed like it was worth watching him. I'm almost at the restaurant. I'll pick you up."

Chapter 43

"There's the old trailer we had years ago." Maggie pointed to the tiny mobile home they had owned when they first married and then finally sold years later. She had no idea why they kept it so long, but they rented it out now and then until one of the renters asked to buy it.

"You think the key is still hanging on the underneath side of the steps?"

"It's worth a try. Let's go find out. If we run into the present owners, I think they'll understand."

The words barely left Maggie's mouth before the rain came down in buckets, and they ran uphill toward the deck attached to the mobile home.

"At least this should put out the fires," Maggie said as Chris pushed her up the steps. He then climbed under to look for the key they hung on a nail his dad had placed there for that reason. He thought of the copperhead snakes that sometimes hid out in dark places like under the deck. Mom always tossed mothballs under there to keep them at bay, but he didn't have time to worry about such things now. He hoped if they were there, they were back farther away from the opening and out of the weather.

And even without the flashlight he wished he'd had several times, he felt until he found the key dangling from the nail and dripping rain. Chris crawled from under the steps and found his mom wet and shivering at the front door.

Miraculously, the old key still fit.

The trailer was dark when he opened the door and stepped in. It smelled musty from lack of use, but it was a welcome shelter.

Flipping on light switches, Maggie moved to the back of the trailer and quickly returned with towels from the bathroom handing one to Chris.

"I'll have to let the owners know we helped ourselves to their place. I'm sure they'll understand. They're only here on the weekends and not all that often, I don't think." Maggie towel dried her hair and then hung the towel on the rack to dry. Rummaging through the cabinets, she emerged with two blankets and handed one to Chris then wrapped up and sat on the old vinyl couch.

Maggie ran her hand over the cool, damp vinyl. "Dad and I bought this old thing used and thought it was just perfect for the trailer. You could sit on it with wet swimsuits. I can't believe it's still here."

"Feels pretty good right now," Chris said, leaning back and rubbing his head.

****

When the thunder hit, Paul instantly had five kids in his lap. The baby softly cried, and her big sister told her it would be okay. Paul nodded and agreed, it would be okay.

Then the lights went out.

"Eric, Emory, stay with the girls while I get a flashlight," Paul said standing and walking toward the kitchen. Bashing his knee on the coffee table, he felt his way in the dark. Why hadn't he thought of this before now and prepared? The answer was because he never expected the weather to get so bad this quickly. He instantly thought of Maggie and his son. But he knew they respected the weather and would put into shore quickly if something happened.

And he was home with scared kids and couldn't go searching.

"It's okay, Sarah," one of the twins could be heard saying in the living room as Paul found the flashlight.

He flipped it on shining it on the kids piled up on the sofa. "Yea! We have light!"

They all giggled—just as the generator came to life and the lights in the house came back on—along with the TV and their movie. It would be okay, Paul thought. To be safe, he'd call Maggie's and Hope's cells and check on them.

And the thunder increased making baby Sarah cry again. Paul reached into the basket of throws Maggie kept next to the sofa and handed around the security blankets scooping Sarah up in a hug. "We'll be okay. The storm won't last too long, I'm sure."

At least he hoped not.

Chapter 44

Saturday a.m.

Again, she heard lapping. Suddenly, Hope's toe touched something slick. Instinctively, she drew her legs up and then both feet slid through the soft grass. Grass grew near the shore. She was near land! She looked up and could just make out trees in the distance, and she realized her knees brushed bottom. She stood and found the log that saved her life was floating near her legs.

She was once more on dry land.

The sandy bottom sank with each step of her feet. She grabbed a stub that stuck out from the log that saved her life and used it as a handle, pulling it with her up on the shore. She was unsure why she wanted to keep her lifesaver, but it gave her comfort to keep it near her. The breeze blew her wet clothes making her shiver even more. But there was shelter ahead.

Once on land she let go of the log she dragged and walked toward the tree line. She had no idea where her sandals were, probably at the bottom of the lake. The rocks and sticks stabbed her bare feet.

But at least she hadn't drowned.

Near the trees Hope sat down with a bush blocking most of the wind. Scooping leaves and sand around and over her like a bum on a park bench, she covered herself with whatever she could find. Slowly the shivering began to subside. When daylight came, she'd find out where she was and try to summon help.

For now, she would stay alive.

Sleep came more easily than she originally thought. Cold, wet, and exhausted, she had scooped as many leaves as possible over her to help insulate against the cold. And now on dry land she dozed in dreamless sleep. Her arm under the uninjured side of her head, she lay on the sandy beach warming slightly—when the rain began.

Earlier in the evening she'd seen lightning in the distance. She thought the weather would move away. She was wrong. Clad only in the sundress she'd worn for tonight cold rain pelted her skin. The wrap she received as a present was still on the boat. Even her sandals were gone.

A loud clap of thunder woke her from the fragile sleep, and she realized a storm approached. She needed more shelter than the leaves provided. Maybe she would stay dryer in the trees. She knew not to move under a tree in a lightning storm but had no idea where else to go. If she stayed here, she'd catch pneumonia.

She stood and looked in the distance as lightning lit up the sky. The rain came down in buckets soaking her to the skin. The thin cotton dress clung to her legs as she ran for the trees, stumbling over rocks and branches along the way, cutting her feet. Under the relative safety of the trees, she saw something tall and dark in the distance. Shelter?

Another bolt of lightning revealed an abandoned pickup rusting in the woods. How it got there she had no idea, but it looked like a savior to her. Hope yanked and pulled on the ancient door handle until it finally it broke free and opened with a loud creak. She climbed in hoping she was the only resident of the pickup and slammed the door closed behind her. Rain fell on the spider-webbed windshield. It smelled of old cigarettes and stale beer, but she didn't care.

A flash of lightning and another clap of thunder soon followed, and she knew the storm was upon her. Then she heard another sound. A loud cracking. Noise thundered behind her shaking the earth. An earthquake? Tornado? What else could she endure tonight? And underneath the sound of the thunder a new sound. A loud sucking noise.

The glass inside the pickup quickly fogged, and she tried in vain to wipe the back window dry with the palm of her hand. She pushed open the door, looked behind her, and could see trees moving in the distance. The generally still water in the lake began to roil, and she wiped her eyes. This could not be.

In lightning strikes she could see the lake roll by like a river, and she knew that was not possible. There was a strong current on the lake that shouldn't be there. Keystone Lake was fed by rivers but didn't have a current.

Thankfully, she was out of the lake and in the relative safety of the old truck. At least she hoped it was safe. What was happening out there? She had nowhere else to go. She watched in horror, mouth ajar, as the water rushed away from the sand. No idea why the lake would begin to move like a white-water river—she knew one thing—the noise she heard wasn't a tornado.

Chapter 45

The compact car slid into the inclined parking lot at the bottom of the dam. He was the only car in the lot and wondered where the night shift employee was. The rains were relentless. Sheets of rain came down sideways as the winds blew. Shipley trudged up the hill, slipping and sliding in worn deck shoes. His head down to avoid the sting of the rain on his face, he climbed the stairs to the top of the dam as quickly as he could. He'd never seen rain like this. Holding the railing with one hand as he climbed, he felt in his pocket with the other hand for the key to the door.

He turned the key and stepped inside the door flipping on a light switch. There was no one here. The industrial fluorescent lights slowly lit the long, dark room. Alone, he'd have to remember what he learned from Decker about how to open the gates. Where was that man, anyway? The noise on the outside of the dam where the lake splashed sounded like thunder. It was unnerving. He quickly flipped switches he thought were correct as another clap of thunder—or wave of water—pounded his ears. He ran. Grabbing the blueprints, stored in the cabinet beside the door, he didn't even switch off the lights or lock the door behind him as he headed once more for the car. The tube of precious prints bounced against his shoulder as he ran down the stairs oblivious of the water splashing around him.

****

The already too-high water from upstream rose to the peak of the berm pressing against the concrete. Even if the dam had been new, the dam would have been in trouble. The trash rack, a heavy-duty screen at the opening of the dam where the water flowed in, held back large debris keeping it from infiltrating the turbines deep inside the concrete structure. But the tiny zebra mussels slipped past with ease. The minute pests attached themselves down the wall of the water-intake, and some slid into the turbines farther into the structure that created hydroelectricity. Soon their shells would impede the workings of the turbine itself.

The Corps of Engineers, aware of the zebra mussels, added chlorine and sulfuric acid to the water to kill the pests, but all it seemed to do was kill off the fish. The mussels had been left unimpeded for too long.

The waves of water crashed onto the lake side of the dam, splashing in the lights of the parking lot. Lightning flash followed by a quick clap of thunder was proof the storm was getting closer.

****

Ryan and Erin watched as the compact car pulled down and into the parking lot of the dam. The rain fell in sheets so hard they could barely see across the road as it filled the lake behind the already-overstressed fifty-year-old dam. Ryan pulled the SUV to the side of the road up the hill from the dam parking lot.

Ryan switched off the engine. “I don’t want him to see my headlights.”

“What is Shipley up to?” Erin asked as they watched from the parked car. “After the conversation I overheard on the phone, I was certain he was the culprit buying up the land around the lake. Do you think he is also responsible for locking up the dam and not allowing the water to flow out? No one wants to own land that's underwater."

Ryan shook her head. "I don't know, but something caused the lake to flood, and the Corps of Engineers met last week to create a plan to fix the problem—much too late."

Erin wiped the inside of the windshield of fog. "I can't see. We've got to get out, rain or no rain."

Stepping out into the blinding rain, Ryan shoved the keys deep into her pocket. Motioning to Erin, she crept down the hill toward the parking lot that sat at the bottom of the dam, her flip flops slipping on the inclined blacktop as she edged closer.

"Did you see that?" Erin asked. A glint of light shone where the door at the top of the concrete monolith opened, then quickly closed. She picked at a thorn in her big toe. Why didn't she change shoes before she started climbing hills? Minutes later, the door swung open, and Shipley stepped out again, quickly running down the stairs. Both women dove for cover under a soggy bush as they watched him run for the safety of his car.

Cavernous groans came from deep inside the dam so loud they could be heard over the roar of the storm. Erin glanced up to the top of the dam. She thought she saw movement and wiped the water from her eyes once more to be sure of what she saw.

The concrete began to quiver. No, that had to be just rainwater in her eyes.

"Oh shit!" Erin watched in horror as a piece fell from the top splashing into the river below. Pressure on the backside of the dam where the water pressed against it continually began to create cracks in the wall and loosen it from the banks that held the dam together. A grinding noise heralded the smaller cracks running together into an even larger one. Then an immense bolt of lightning lit up the sky once more, hitting the transformers attached to the turbine and running through the structure.

Both women jumped. “Come on!” Erin shouted over the roar of the storm and quickly began to climb the hill back to the road. Lightning lit up the turbulent night sky illuminating the ever-widening crack.

Suddenly the giant turbine ground to a halt. Erin stopped and looked behind her. The lack of noise from the turbines was unworldly, and she stared gaped-mouth—rain blinding her.

Once in his car, Shipley squealed tires as he rushed toward the top of the slippery incline. The lightweight car slid sideways on the wet, steep asphalt.

Erin was no longer worried about the danger of being seen by the man. The danger of the water was much greater. She grabbed Ryan’s arm as they climbed back onto the road and then over the other side into the trees as fast as their bodies would go. Erin’s legs screamed at the exertion they didn’t get sitting at her desk. She climbed higher glancing behind her hearing tires slide on the wet pavement. Rain ran like a river down the concrete and into the river below. The car wasn’t gaining much ground.

Shipley was in trouble.

The roar was gradual but soon could be heard even over the thunder. Locals probably thought it was a tornado coming across the prairie that sounded like a freight train. The ground shook as the water crashed against the concrete that held it back for years. Erin clung to a slender pine tree feeling the vibration under her and then climbed even faster up the hill using her arms and legs pulling her toward the car.

The giant dam crumbled slowly at first, picking up speed as it collapsed, rolling into the Arkansas River. Lake Keystone rushed over the top of the rubble, and blue-green water gushed downstream foaming into white caps racing toward Tulsa and points below. Erin knew all in the path of the river were in mortal danger as the water was sucked from the lake into the river running downstream toward the heavily populated area of Tulsa. She thought of Aunt Toni and wondered where she was tonight, but she had no idea. She'd try to call as soon as she was safe.

Ryan allowed herself time to spin around once more and pointed downhill. Erin turned in time to witness Shipley's car, unable to climb the slick hill, washing into the monstrous river—its occupant still inside.

Boulders from both sides began to slide into the lake that once kept out the water. They climbed faster no matter what their legs said, the bank crumbling behind them.

Back out onto the road and out of the trees, they ran with their heads down, hiding from what Erin didn't know. Was she afraid the lake would see her and come after her? The only other witness to the catastrophe was already swept away.

Pulling the keys from her pocket, Ryan crawled into her SUV as Erin got in the passenger's side. She made a fast U-turn on wet pavement—sliding as she forced the car to climb the hill. The monstrous dam crumbled behind them, and the road to the dam fell into the water as the vehicle raced toward the highway.

Erin was afraid to look behind her.

Once back on the highway, she tried to call Rob, her mother, Aunt Toni, and Bernadette. She couldn't get through to anyone.

Chapter 46

Paul tried not to show his concern for Chris and Maggie. So far the kids were glued to the TV and the generator kept the electricity going. He'd dialed Maggie and Chris' cell phones and also 911, but there was no answer. Lines must be down. He was home alone with five kids and couldn't leave to go look for his wife or son. He had to keep it together, he thought. What would he tell them if no one came home?

He'd also tried to reach Hope, but she must have shut her phone off for the evening. Normally she called in several times to check on the kids, but it was a special evening. Their seventh anniversary. It seemed ages since he and Maggie had a seventh anniversary. That was many years ago. They hadn't even built the house they lived in now.

The boom of thunder shook the house, and both sets of twins instantly climbed on the couch with him. Baby Sarah slept comfortably in his lap. She jumped in her sleep but still didn't wake. To be that young and unworried by the world…

Then the sucking noise began. It sounded like a giant sink emptying after a clog was relieved. No, it was unlike anything Paul had ever heard—and it was coming from the lake. All heads swiveled toward the deck.

"Stay here," Paul said to the children and ran for the back door. Of course, they were all right behind him.

Once he was out on the deck, he realized he still held the sleeping baby—and it was raining. The cover over the deck kept most of it off, but they'd all be wet soon. He flipped on the lights to the outside of the house and the one on the dock where the boat would be tied—if Chris and Maggie hadn't taken it out.

In the distance he could see the dock sway in the breeze. It groaned, and a deep ripping noise was heard. A crack of lightning flashed showing the dock being torn from its moorings and racing away as if towed—as the light on the dock went out and he could see no more. But he was certain the water had a current and it was what pulled the dock away. What else could have done it? A current! Lakes didn't have currents, at least not whitewater rapids. It wasn't a river.

Hearing sobbing, he realized the baby in his arms wasn't the only child on the deck with him. They all surrounded him and saw the destruction too. He had to get them inside and dry. And he had to do it now.

"Okay, everybody back inside." He nodded to the door that stood open with rain blowing in.

"I'm scared," Jill cried and grabbed his leg.

"Me too, sweetie, let's go inside where it is warm and dry, and we won't be scared anymore."

Ushering kids in the door, Paul saw movement off the end of deck coming their way.

"Grandma!" Both sets of twins ran for the steps, and Paul turned in time to see his wife and son walking in as the rain pelted down.

"Oh, it's so good to see you!" Maggie sobbed, and Paul leaned over huddled children to hug his wife while holding a crying baby. Then he hugged his son who took Sarah from his arms.

"Where have you been? We were so worried. Where's the boat, and did you see what the lake just did?" Paul's questions came out as one long sentence.

Chris wrapped the baby tighter in the soggy blanket. "We just got here. I don't know what you mean, but we heard a weird sucking noise coming from the water. What was that?"

Once more the torrential rain ceased, and only a light sprinkle remained. Paul glanced down the hill where his boat dock should be and then stepped inside the door coming back with a flashlight and gestured toward the water. Walking down the pathway that led to the boat dock, Chris and Paul felt their way along guided by the small light through wet grass. Maggie followed behind watching the children in the damp vegetation to be sure no one fell. The rain had quit, but the moon, covered by clouds, gave little light to go by. They were dependent upon the small flashlight.

"That was the weirdest thing I've ever seen. It looked like there was a current to the water, and then the boat dock broke off and the lights went out. I think it floated downstream! Then you and your mother came home." Paul had no idea why he felt he had to explain himself.

In the dark, Paul thought he could see the mooring posts sticking out of the water. But they sat much higher than usual.

"Dad, are those the moorings?" Chris grabbed his father's arm and pointed out into the water. "Where's the water?"

Paul stood where the grass quit and shone his light out into the lake waving it slowly back and forth. Taking a branch he found on the ground, he gingerly stuck it out and touched mud. The moorings sticking out from the bank stood taller than his head. This was not his boat dock. But it had to be. This path only led to one dock. His neighbors had their own docks and pathways to them.

The men looked at each other in the dark barely able to see expressions on each other's faces. "This can't be," Paul began. "But Chris, what I saw before you arrived looked like the water was rushing downstream. And there was that loud sucking noise—like all the water was being sucked out of the lake."

"I heard it too when Mom and I were walking, just before we got here. I had no idea what it was."

"Hey Paul," a voice from down the bank called. "Is that you? What happened to the water? Do you think the dam broke?"

Paul and Chris turned to see a man making his way toward them along the bank. Allen White stumbled down the path that once led near the water and joined the two properties.

"Allen? That was some strange noise we heard earlier." Paul shaded his eyes as the neighbor came toward them with a flood light in his hand. The neighbor lowered the light and walked up extending his hand.

Allen nodded then shone his light out into the lake. "I can't believe this," he said. From what they could see in the dark, the area of the lake was nothing but mud.

No water, just mud.

"I've never seen anything like it." Chris stared out past the moorings.

Paul shone his own small light back and forth as they all stood in silence. "The dam must have broken. I hope the bad weather had everyone off the lake." And then it hit him. "What about Tulsa?"

Suddenly the air was full of sirens—most of them were far away, some closer, as first responders raced down the road toward town.

"What could have caused the lake to do that?" Paul said to anyone who listened. Then he again tried 911. He got no response.

Allen once more spoke. "I'll tell you what did it. That dam broke just like we told them it would. I'm going back to the house. You folks might as well do the same. We can't do anything about this." Allen spoke and then turned taking his flood light back toward his cabin leaving the Becks with a small flashlight.

The sirens continued. "Goodnight, Allen. Be safe," Paul called after the older man. "Either the towers are down, or they just aren't answering calls right now. But we need to get these kids inside." They climbed back up the hill to the house. Once inside, Paul put his damp phone on the table.

Chris reached for two dish towels and handed one to his mother as he wiped his face with the other. Sarah cried softly and snuggled into his wet chest.

"Where have you two been all this time?" Paul looked first at one and then the other covered in mud and scratches in jackets that belonged to someone else.

Maggie looked at Chris, then she spoke. "There was a little accident, and I think we may be buying a new boat. But we're all here and safe, that's what matters. Thank goodness we weren't on the water when the dam broke."

"Accident? Boating accident? Are you okay?" Paul looked at his wife and son.

"We hit some rocks in the high water, Dad. The boat

is in splinters. I'll pay for it. I was driving and distracted by the fires on the other side of the lake. But I don't think either of us are hurt. Mom twisted an ankle, but it seems okay. At least she's not limping right now." He gently touched his head. "My head has quit bleeding. We broke into the old trailer and borrowed these jackets after we rested a while. Then we walked the rest of the way here."

"I need some coffee," Maggie said and stepped to the sink to fill the pot, children clung to her legs.

"They've been worried about Grandma," Paul said.

"And Ted and Hope?" Chris raised an eyebrow in question.

"It's their anniversary, and I doubt we'll hear from them. They were planning on the kids spending the night, and they know where they are. Likely, they're cuddled up safe and dry." Paul reached into the cabinet for mugs. "And I might have some hot chocolate here in the cabinet too." It occurred to Paul the kids never did have dinner, just snacks. "Who's hungry?" he said sticking his head in the fridge to find something to eat. Glancing out the window he saw the sky begin a light shade of pink. It would soon be morning.

Maggie started the coffee as headlights from the gravel drive lit up the house. It was the sheriff's cruiser pulling into the driveway.

"Maybe he has some news," Paul said and walked back onto the deck.

The sheriff stepped out of the driver's side door just as the passenger door opened. A small person stepped out.

It looked like Hope—covered in mud.

The whole family bolted for the door. Hope, with a dress stained in mud and hair disheveled, wobbled toward the deck.

“Momma!” the kids shouted in unison and ran to her.

“Hey, Becks.” The sheriff trotted toward the family. “I found this little lady on the road. She needed a ride. And she had a fantastic story to tell me along the way. I’ll be back to take a statement, but she’s safe now, and I have to get to town to find out what just happened to our lake. A lot of people are depending upon it.”

“Thank you, Sheriff,” Hope said with a weak voice and walked toward the house with her arms around her children.

Chapter 47

Saturday a.m. as daylight breaks

Hope was happy for the clothes Mom found for her to wear after she took a shower. Pulling herself away from the kids with promises to not be long, she used the shower in her parents' bedroom while Chris used the front bathroom. Maggie washed up in the kitchen.

Dad prepared bacon and eggs for them as the sun came up, and everyone ate a little. The kids were tired and grumpy and barely let their mother go long enough for her to clean up.

Hope had promised to tell her parents and brother the story as soon as the kids were asleep. She had no idea what to say to the kids—but that could come later. She looked in the mirror at the bruised and battered face and knew she was lucky to be alive. She wondered where Ted was. Did he get off the lake before the dam broke? Did she really care?

Walking down the hall in her mother's clothes that were too big, she thought it really didn't matter. She was clean and dry—and alive. And the bacon smelled heavenly.

"Um, bacon." Hope hugged her father as he set a plate on the table for her. She had difficulty letting go of the safety of the man who raised her. How would he react when he knew the full story? And Chris? Ted had better hope the police got to him before her family did. If he was still alive. She warmed her hands on the coffee cup and sipped slowly. Her cheek still hurt from the blow she received last night. Was that only last night? It seemed a week ago.

Maggie was cuddling Sarah with her bottle, but the baby was fussy, and Hope took her. The child instantly relaxed as soon as she felt her mother's touch and was asleep in no time. But Hope was in no hurry to put her down. Eating while holding a baby had become second nature to Hope. Then she realized the other children were asleep on the pallet in the living room. The TV on, and food in their stomachs, not to mention the excitement of last night, was too much.

It was time. Her family had kept quiet glancing at her now and then.

"Why don't we take this out on the deck?" Hope handed the baby off to Maggie who laid the child in her playpen in the living room. Paul held the door open for Hope to step out on the deck where Chris had already dried off patio chairs.

In the full sunlight of the morning, they all looked out into what used to be a body of water—but was now a lake of mud and debris. The soil at the bottom of that lake had been covered with water for so long it was now a bog. If you tried to walk out on it, you might sink up to your waist.

"I never thought I'd see this." Paul leaned on the deck railing with coffee in hand. "The lake-front property your mom and I bought for a home is now mud-front property."

"But we're all alive to talk about it." Maggie sat at the table. The others joined her.

"So," Chris began. "Mom and I wrecked the boat last night and are lucky to be alive. Hope, you going to tell us what happened to you?"

Hope instantly teared up. She dabbed at her eyes with the napkin she brought with her. She might need a lot more before she was done.

She took a deep breath. "I ended up in the water last night. Took a fall from the boat, that Ted had borrowed for us. I floated on a log for a while—like you and I used to, Chris, when we were kids. I was lucky it came along. Then when I floated to the bank, I found an old, abandoned pickup to get into when the storm hit. I got in it for a while then I heard the loud noise from the lake. I couldn't imagine what that was. We all know now that the dam broke, and the lake flowed downstream. Those poor people in Tulsa! When it quit raining and was getting light, I realized I wasn't far from a road. When I got there the sheriff came by. He was in a hurry to get to the emergency situations in town, but he stopped to pick me up. Then he dropped me off here."

"You have a boat?" Chris asked leaning on the chair he had turned around backward. Mom used to hate it when he did that as a kid.

"No, Ted borrowed it. He wants to buy it, but there is no way."

"So where is Ted now, and how did you end up in the water?" Chris' eyes were narrowed, and it was obvious he was becoming agitated.

Paul cleared his throat. "Hope, you grew up on a lake and know how to take care of yourself on a boat, how did you just fall in, and where was Ted in all of this? You floated on a log? He didn't pull you back in?"

"He was drunk. We were fighting—I mean arguing.

He wanted to buy the boat, and the bank has been calling about overdue bills now. I said there was no way we could buy the boat. For some reason—I guess it was the alcohol—he just became enraged. He slapped me and I almost passed out. The next thing I knew I was flying through the air and hit the water. I called to him, but he must not have realized I was not on the boat. He drove away." She had no idea why she was trying to defend the man who tried to kill her—well she could think of five reasons.

Chris stood, knocking the chair over. "He threw you off the boat and drove away?"

Maggie reached for his hand, and he jerked away. "Quiet, Chris, the kids."

"The kids! They'll know soon enough. I wonder where he ended up with the rented boat when the lake went dry? I hope he was washed down stream with the rest of the debris! How big was the boat?" Chris had not quieted down. His eyes blazed.

Then Hope glanced at her father, and he was beet red. "What did the boat look like? Where on the lake were you?" he had his cell phone in his hand and was ready to dial. "We'll find him. He'll pay for what he did to you. He'll never see his kids again and will surely do jail time."

Maggie patted Hope's arm. "Hope, all this was over an argument about money?"

"He was really drunk. He's been doing a lot more of that lately, and I'm sure he'd had some before we went out. Then there was wine on the boat. He said I'd always had money and didn't know what it was like not to. He was never going to be poor again. He was ranting out of his mind."

"Yeah, he's out of his mind, all right, if he thinks he can get away with murder—or attempted murder—in this family." Chris paced the deck.

An SUV pulled into the drive as the argument was heating up, and Ryan climbed out from the driver's side, then Erin from the passenger's.

Hope saw Chris instantly relax when he saw Ryan.

But Ryan was not relaxed. She and Erin ran up the steps and then stopped when they saw Hope.

Ryan looked like the cat that ate the canary. "Hi, I guess everyone is okay here. We wanted to be sure the family was safe and sound—you know since the phones are down." She calmed herself walking toward Chris.

"We're all alive," Chris said. "It was an eventful night." He put an arm around Ryan and nodded at Erin.

Silence hung in the air.

"I'll get the coffee." Maggie headed to the kitchen, and Paul found chairs for the guests.

"Returning with a thermos and two more cups, Maggie set it on the picnic table, then poured the brown liquid into mugs. No one spoke.

Erin reached for a cup and took a sip. "This is heaven, Maggie. Thank you. We too had an eventful night. I'm sure everyone on the lake did."

Chris pulled a chair close to him for Ryan to sit in. "Yeah, Mom and I had a boating accident, but both walked away from it. The boat is toast. That was before all the water in the lake ran downstream. Any news on Tulsa yet?"

Erin spoke first. "Rob's fine. He talked to Mom and my Aunt Toni. They were both in Mannford and also Bernadette and her family. Luckily, none of them were in Tulsa. There must be substantial damage there, lives lost."

Paul cleared his throat. "We've talked to the Corps of Engineers people about the dam for some time. Now with all the flooding and then the storm, I guess it was just too much to take."

"Yes, we're all lucky today." Erin sipped her coffee again. "Hope, were you in the boating accident too? You've got quite a shiner there."

And the tears that had threatened to fall earlier became a flood as Hope told her story once again.

"He pushed you off the boat and left you?" Ryan's eyes looked like Chris'.

She shoved her fiery red hair behind her ear and nodded.

Chris, who had been quiet, looked up and clenched his hands into fists. "And I'm gonna find him." He stood and walked toward the house then paused, slapping his forehead with one hand. "Can I borrow the car again?"

"I'll come with you." Paul pulled the keys from his pocket and tossed them to Chris. "We can start at the marina that rents boats. If it's still standing."

"He's not at the marina, Paul." All eyes were suddenly on Erin.

"You know where he is, and you didn't say anything?" Paul's face became darker.

"Sit down, and I'll tell you the whole story," Erin began.

Chris remained standing as she told the people on the patio of Ryan seeing Ted come in on the boat and then following him to the dam in the storm. She said he went into the dam and then returned with a tube in his hand. Then she stopped and took a deep breath.

"His car sat in the flooded parking lot at the base of

the dam. And it couldn't get enough traction trying to come up the hill in the rain. The dam was breaking apart behind him and he—he didn't make it out. He was swept away."

"He was swept away in the car. You mean he could still be alive?" Hope's red eyes squeezed a few more tears from them, tears she didn't know she still had.

"I don't think he'd survive that, Hope. I'm sorry." Ryan walked over and put an arm around the woman as she sobbed. Slowly she began to stop and looked up at Ryan. "You saw him come in on the boat. Why did that make you follow him?"

Ryan looked at Erin then back at Hope. Erin spoke first. "Hope, we've been looking into the activity of T & H Realty." She paused. "We've looked at all the property around the lake that has sold lately, and one name kept coming up, T & H Realty, LLC. All the properties that sold, some without an advertisement, and people just up and disappearing, made us look into the situation. Maybe T & H Realty did those people a favor by buying their flooded property, but I doubt it. They all sold for pennies on the dollar. Those people were robbed."

Hope nodded, wondering what was coming next.

"T & H Realty, LLC is owned by Ted and Hope Shipley, I guess you know that."

Hope shook her head. "Chris and I talked about this. Ted and I don't own a realty company, and we can barely pay the monthly mortgage on our own home, let alone others."

"The company is owned by Ted and Hope Shipley, and we have Ted's signature on paperwork that set up the LLC. Only one signature is required, and it definitely looks like Ted's signature. And the address of the LLC is your home."

Hope realized her mouth was falling open more all the time. Could it be true? Could Ted have put them in this position? Her head swirled. He'd tried to kill her—left her to drown. She was probably a widow with five small children. And now this—a ton of debt, and no job.

She hoped he was dead.

Chapter 48

Monday after dam break

In the light of day, the damage to Tulsa was visible. Homes were destroyed and many washed away. The death toll was rising, and news helicopters swarmed the sky.

Erin thanked God her family was in Mannford instead of Tulsa when the disaster hit. She and Aunt Toni would be living at Mom's for a while, since getting into Tulsa and the office was almost impossible. Rob found his way back to their apartment from Mannford on back roads with his four-wheel-drive Jeep and brought the essentials back with him. He was happy to report that the flooding didn't affect the apartment complex. Mom moved in with Brent, so Erin, Rob and Toni could live at her house.

Erin's car still sat parked at the floating restaurant—that no longer floated.

Erin's phone chimed, and Ryan's face showed up on her phone. "Hey, you need your car? I can come get you and take to you to get it out of the parking lot at Pier 51."

"Oh, could you? That would be great," Erin replied. Ryan was becoming someone who had once been an acquaintance and now a good friend. Risking your life together had that effect on a relationship.

"Follow me back to Mom's if you have time. I want

to show you something," Erin said when Ryan dropped her off at her car. In the passenger's seat lay her laptop with all the info gathered on T & H Realty. The same sad old laptop she'd always used—the one with the dent in the top and the letter "E" rubbed off the keyboard. It was an old friend. They'd been through a lot together. After an incident several years ago with the stolen laptop, she backed it up. She always kept a second copy of everything.

Erin and Ryan sat at her mother's kitchen table—the one Erin had grown up around. She'd shared meals there with her mom and dad. Later Aunt Toni and her mother had spent nights there laughing around guacamole and margaritas on the weekends. The family table was scratched and used—but sacred. She wouldn't take a million dollars for it. And today, it was a desk piled with documents.

"Okay I have copies of the Articles of Organization for the LLC, and there is only one signature, Shipley's. He was also the Registered Agent. That way if anyone sued the company, he would be the one who was served." Erin slid the copy of the document to Ryan to look over.

"Yeah, pretty slick," Ryan said tossing it aside. "That way Hope didn't know what he was up to."

"Yes and no. As Registered Agent, he would be served if there was a lawsuit, and Hope wouldn't have to know about it. But at the same time, her name isn't on here anywhere, only her initial on the name of the LLC, not her name. So, I don't see how she can be responsible for his debt. And under the circumstances, that's a good thing. The debt belongs to the LLC. At least that's how I'd argue it."

Erin's phone rang and the contact said, *Creek*

County Sheriff. Erin had his number in her contacts after all that had happened lately. "Hi, Sheriff Montgomery."

"Hey, Erin. I called with some news."

Erin picked up the pencil and began to take notes on the legal pad beside her.

The sheriff resumed, "With the water subsiding, the Corps has found a ton of things left behind. One was the compact car with the body of Ted Shipley. Inside the car along with the body was a tube that held some interesting blueprints for a massive hotel and marina. I guess that's what he planned to build on the land he stole. I just contacted the family before I called you."

"I assumed he didn't make it. I'm sorry for Hope, though. Blueprints, huh? Any idea where this hotel was to be built?"

"I'd be willing to bet along the area of the land he was buying up, the island where the rivers ran together."

The sheriff was quiet a moment and then spoke again. "And Shipley wasn't the only one. Along the banks of where the lake used to be, there is a lot of debris. One was a car with a body in the trunk that hadn't been there too long. We know he died before the dam break because of decomposition. It had been there longer than Shipley. But he turned out to be a local who owned a bait shop around here. I'm sure a lot of people wondered what happened to the proprietor of Buddy Mac's Bait and Tackle."

"I didn't know he was missing. But I remember him having that store when I was growing up."

Erin could hear the sheriff sigh. "I think a lot of people just thought he up and left town. Anyway, his skull was caved in, and he was placed in the trunk of the car along with the shovel that probably did the deed. I don't think that was an accident."

"No, probably not."

"When I talked to Hope today, she told me there was a guy who called the house now and then. He always asked for Ted and said he was Decker from the dam."

"Decker, huh. Yeah, he was on our radar." Erin was still looking over documents. "I told you I met him and got a weird vibe off him. He was the night shift at the dam. Somehow this doesn't surprise me."

"You've got an instinct, girl. So, I contacted the Corps of Engineers and found Neil Decker who worked at the dam. He kept an eye on gauges and things for the Corps at night. So, I tracked him down. Obviously, he's not working at the dam anymore since the dam is gone, but I went to see him. He was nervous to see me coming. I've gotten pretty good at reading people after all these years and when I mentioned Ted Shipley, he just spilled his guts without a lot of prodding. It seemed he planned to leave the Corps and go to work for Shipley as soon as possible. They'd been falsifying documents and saying the water was being let out faster than it was, and he might have had a little something to do with zebra mussels being added to the dam workings to help it clog faster. When I pressed him, he admitted to breaking into the lab and helping himself to a bucket of mussels. He was an accomplice all right. He wasn't there the night of the storm, though, had an alibi, a stomach bug. He said his roommate would vouch for that. Anyway, if he had been there when the dam broke, he wouldn't have been alive to tell about it."

Erin put down her pencil. "So, he helped Shipley clog the dam even more and not let the water out as quickly as the documents said. All so Shipley could buy up land that was underwater and at a cheaper price."

"Yes, we've said that all along, though we didn't know who it was at first. And I didn't know that the aging dam had any help—with the addition of the zebra mussels and all the water behind it, the collapse was bound to happen. That was creative."

Erin twisted the pencil in her hand thinking. "No one would have even realized if he hadn't spilled the beans. Well, except for all that creative detective work by the sheriff."

Montgomery laughed. "Most criminals aren't very smart. That's why they lead a life of crime." There was silence on the other end of the line for a moment. "Before I talked to Mr. Decker, I asked around a little about him and found he frequented a bar around here. I can't remember the name, used to be called The Thirsty Turtle. I don't know the name now, it's had several. Anyway, in talking to the bartender he'd been in there a few weeks ago drinking and bragging to some other drunk about something he'd done. It seems he might have had something to do with Jeff's death too. The bartender has listened to stories from drunks long enough not to believe all of them. Jeff had come by the dam and had seen the bucket of zebra mussels and wanted to know what they were for. They joked about the fact that a clogged dam with all the flooding was not what the aging dam needed. He said it as a joke. But he wasn't sure that Beck found it funny. He said he might have put a little something in the commuter cup when they were to go out fishing. But Decker didn't want to be there when the deed happened, so he backed out of the fishing trip that night. No one would ever know—he hoped."

Erin put down the pencil and ran a hand through her

hair. "So, Jeff was murdered. Can you pin his death on Decker?"

The sheriff paused and then resumed. "Maybe with a little more evidence. You know I also wondered about the new guy at the dam—Rogers. I talked to him, and he too was concerned about the dam. I think he was telling me the truth about his conversation with Decker. He'd talked to him about the amount of water being let out of the dam at night while Decker was on duty. Decker assured him he was letting it out as planned, but the gauges were old and didn't always work the way they should. He said he was doing his job. Rogers also said he'd seen Shipley's car at the dam at night a lot. He wondered why, but assumed Decker and Shipley were friends and as long as the job got done, he didn't care."

"What a twisted mess. All because of greed."

"Money is the root of all evil—my grandmother used to say that a lot. Of course, she didn't have a penny and wouldn't have known what to do with it if she did. But she was probably right."

The kitchen where Erin sat became noisy. People poured in the back door. "She probably was. Thank you for calling, Sheriff. If there is anything I can do, please let me know." Erin hung up the phone just as the noise became deafening. Aunt Toni came in singing an ABBA tune with a giant bowl of something green and started to place it on the table. Behind her came Erin's mom and Brent.

"Okay, this isn't a desk, move this stuff out of here and make way for the party!" Toni plopped down the glass bowl of green goo and shoved the documents aside.

"Is that guacamole?" Erin asked stacking the documents into a pile and closing her computer. Erin knew better than to try to shut down a party instigated by her aunt.

"It's guacamole and margarita time!" Toni danced to the fridge and pulled out the ice maker bin while her mom plugged in the blender.

Ryan helped find a bowl for the chips, and Erin pulled Aunt Toni aside.

"The sheriff just called. Shipley's body was found still in his car where it had washed downstream. And he had an accomplice per Hope, Neil Decker. Decker told the sheriff everything. He even admitted to stealing the zebra mussels from the lab and dumping them into the dam to help clog it up faster. He wasn't at the dam the night it broke, he has an alibi, but he admitted to being in on it. He's been arrested. Oh, and the sheriff talked to a bartender who overheard Decker saying he put the poison in Jeff's drink. Jeff was murdered—if the sheriff can prove it."

Toni thoughtfully took a bite of the chip in her hand and instantly became serious. "So, he could be charged with murder if it can be proven. Also, conspiracy to defraud. That's a felony and worth up to ten years. And maybe first or second-degree manslaughter for all the people who died in the flooding, culpable negligence, another felony up to life in prison. Grand larceny, another felony. Then there are the Environmental Protection Agency laws that can get him sent to federal prison. It might also fit within the definition of terrorism, given that it was a dam. Wow, that guy will never see the light of day!"

The noise of the blender made it impossible to talk, and they walked back to the kitchen where Brent was hogging the bowl of guacamole.

When the back door opened, Rob walked in with Bernadette beside him. Erin knew she was alive but hadn't seen her since the dam break. She folded her into her arms and hugged her tightly feeling the tiny baby bump that Bernadette often touched protectively. She was alive and so was the tiny being growing inside her.

"Hey, lady. Do babies like guacamole?" Erin asked her friend.

"Probably. It looks like baby food. Where is it?" She bounced in the kitchen toward the bowl on the table.

Erin knew that Bernadette would make an awesome mom.

Chapter 49

Chris and Ryan stood on his parents' deck staring out into what used to be the lake behind their house. It was an odd scene, a muddy mess. But having known the lake all his life, Chris couldn't imagine it wouldn't come back to its former glory—someday. They'd wait.

He looked at Ryan and reached down taking her hand. "I know while we were in college I got cold feet and ran. I don't know if you can forgive me." He paused and looked at the woman he knew he loved more than anything in the world. "But I've decided I've seen the world, and I want to come home. I want to put down roots here on the lake." He kissed her hand. "And if you are still interested, I'd like you to join me." Chris stood holding Ryan's hand. She looked him in the eye and raised one eyebrow.

"Stay here? Forever?"

"Yes, and with you. If you'll have me."

"You're serious? What will you do in Oklahoma?"

"I don't know. Open up a photography studio? I can branch out and do nature photography here as well as other things. A good photographer is always in need. So, what do you say? Are you willing to give me another chance?"

Ryan squealed and threw her arms around him. "Yes! Oh, I've missed you—no, I've missed us." She pressed her lips to his and lingered there until he responded in a passionate kiss—as the door opened and his parents walked out with a tray of drinks.

"I'm sorry, we didn't mean to interrupt," Paul said trying to push Maggie back inside.

"No, you're not interrupting," Chris said. "Ryan and I were just discussing our future, and I want you here. I've decided to stay in Mannford. I have to go back to finish what I was working on. I might be gone a few weeks, but then I'll be back for good." He smiled at Ryan and then his parents. Placing his hand on her chin he turned her facing him. "Do you want to go with me? Do you have vacation time?"

"I'll make time," she responded and kissed him again.

"I, for one, think this is wonderful," Maggie said sitting at the table and gesturing for them to join her.

"Both of us," Paul said. "I'm thrilled to be able to see my son more and his girlfriend."

Chris smiled. "Or wife, if she'll have me."

Ryan paused. "Let's take this slowly. Okay? First, let's get you back home where you belong." She kissed him again, and they sat at the table as Maggie handed around glasses of iced tea.

"That's wonderful. And I'm sorry this isn't champagne, but I was unprepared," then she leaned across the table and hugged her son and Ryan.

The conversation slowed, and they all stared across the mud at the sun setting behind trees.

Maggie wrapped her arm around Paul and laid her head on his shoulder before settling down to watch the sunset on her lake.

Whatever condition it was in, Chris thought, it was still his lake, and his family was once again together to enjoy it.

****

The lakebed began to dry up. The river that still flowed in the middle of where the lake used to be was the only water. Maggie walked down the pathway to where the dock once sat and looked out at the mud that now cracked and baked in the sun. She was still afraid to walk on the lakebed that appeared dry but might suck her down. A small river of water ran down the middle of the cove where she once swam—the Arkansas river still flowed. It would someday be dammed up again filling her beautiful lake one more time. It might be years she reminded herself. Rome wasn't built in a day, and neither was the Keystone Lake dam—not the first or the second time. She wished Jeff could see this. He'd be amazed—everyone was. But she'd bet Jeff was looking down from heaven, with Cher by his side, at the lake they both loved.

Erin and Rob went home to their apartment leaving Mom to return home. Much of Tulsa was still drying out, but they were some of the lucky ones. The loss of property was small in comparison to the loss of life.

Sheriff Montgomery drove past the area where the yachts were docked. Many were now sitting in the sand, listing to the left and partially sunk in silt. *All In* could be seen painted on the back of one encrusted in the sandy bottom. All the other names were covered by sand.

At the dam site workers toiled day and night to once again restore the beautiful dam that provided not just electricity and water to the city downstream, but recreation for everyone to enjoy. The lights were on twenty-four hours as the night shift took over to work on the building of the dam. The rains had finally stopped completely. No more mid-afternoon showers or midnight storms. Mother Nature had made herself known in the spring and early summer and finally decided to rest and let the dam be built once more.

The sheriff looked across the banks of the Arkansas river from one side to the other. It was the area where the Arkansas and Cimarron rivers ran together and dumped sand and water into the lake. This was the place once called the islands where boaters partied and sometimes became a peninsula if they'd had a dry year. Now it was sand—drier in some places than others. It was cordoned off to keep the kids on four-wheelers from interfering with the work going on at the dam. Shore birds still ran across the sand sometimes looking confused wondering where the water went. In the distance he could see a blue heron on a fishing expedition in the trickle of river that still ran. The sheriff surveyed the area and wondered where Shipley had planned the resort to be built. It was a beautiful place and would be again someday.

And in the ending light of day, he saw something shiny yards from where the bank once sat—it looked like a shard of pottery. He rolled up his pant legs and gently walked across the sand and mud, his shoes barely sinking. Leaning down he gently picked up the pot that lay on its side. The dammed rivers that became a lake once covered the town of Keystone, but this was older than the lake. He picked it up gently and turned it over flaking the mud from its sides. At one time the Yachee and Creek Indian tribes lived here before the white settlement and later the damming of the rivers. The pot was not complete, but it would make an archeologist salivate. He'd take it to someone at the university who might know, but it looked like a Native American pot from long before the lake was dammed and had probably been underwater for years. It reminded him that this land had been many things before it was a lake.

An eagle screeched overhead, and he looked up. A small population of eagles wintered at Keystone Lake for years. Maybe they would begin to nest here again as the lake returned to its glory. Once again nature was reclaiming its land.

The lake was still there, only in a different form. And it would return again—in spite of the greed that tried to destroy it—because of the people who lived there and loved it.

A word about the author…

Peggy Chambers calls Enid, Oklahoma home. She has been writing for several years and is a multi-genre published author, always working on another. She has two children, five grandchildren and lives with her husband and dog. She attended Phillips University, the University of Central Oklahoma and is a graduate of the University of Oklahoma. She is a member of the Enid Writers' Club and Oklahoma Writers' Federation, Inc. There is always another story weaving itself around in her brain trying to come out. There aren't enough hours in the day!

You can find her at http://peggylchambers.com/ where she writes a weekly blog, like her on Facebook at https://www.facebook.com/BraWars, connect with her on Twitter at @authorpeggycham, or Instagram at champeggy.

http://peggylchambers.com/

Thank you for purchasing
this publication of The Wild Rose Press, Inc.

For questions or more information
contact us at
info@thewildrosepress.com.

The Wild Rose Press, Inc.
www.thewildrosepress.com

www.ingramcontent.com/pod-product-compliance
Lightning Source LLC
LaVergne TN
LVHW050617100826
845148LV00011B/1629

* 9 7 8 1 5 0 9 2 4 0 2 5 8 *